EGGNOG IN AMESBURY

(CHRISTMAS IN AMESBURY SERIES)

TRACY BROEMMER

Eggnog in Amesbury

by

Tracy Broemmer

Contemporary Romance Novella

Published by Tracy Broemmer

Edited by Lexie Broemmer

Cover by Zakzrewski Designs

All Rights Reserved

ISBN#: 978-1-951637-78-1

For Mr. Allison

~Your Facebook message to me on August 6, 2018

"Happy Birthday

Tracy you have a great day and enjoy writing and write one for Hallmark Channel."

Well, it's not the Hallmark Channel, but here's my take on a Hallmark Christmas movie.

Merry Christmas to you and your family, Mr. Allison!

CHAPTER ONE

MCKENZIE

Traffic on this highway was nonexistent. Good thing for her. McKenzie Noble had belted out the last four songs at the top of her lungs. She would be exhausted by the time she reached Amesbury. Not that she cared. A music fan in general, she *loved* Christmas music. And why not blare it if she was alone in her rental car on the drive? No one to complain about her singing off-key, and no one to pass her and notice her Grammy-Award winning concert.

She checked the time again. When she landed in Missoula, she had been worried she would be late for this meeting. A heavy blanket of dark, mean-looking clouds hung low in the sky, but so far, only tiny flakes of snow fell, adding to that already on the ground here in Montana. The highway itself was clear, so as long as those clouds held off cutting loose with their fury until she reached Amesbury, she would be okay.

Three weeks into her new job, she couldn't afford messing anything up. The position at Inovial Educational Consulting was her first *real* job, as her younger brother would say, even though she had graduated from college six years ago. While she didn't mind waitressing, and yes, she had made good tip money, McKenzie was aware that her parents hadn't put her through college to work at Creighton's for the rest of her life.

Her mom had balked at the idea of her flying to Missoula by herself, but McKenzie was thrilled at the opportunity. Not to mention, she was twenty-seven years old and had lived on her own since she had left home for college. The scouting trip, as her boss Lena had called it, was a perfect chance for her to prove herself at work and an opportunity to see Montana—more than what she had seen in the ridiculously popular TV show, *Yellowstone*.

Now, if she happened to run into a good-looking cowboy or two while she was here, she wouldn't complain. But she wasn't on the lookout for one, either. McKenzie wanted the traditional life her mom had; she wanted to get married and have kids. But right now, she needed to focus on her career. Maybe once she was settled at IEC, she would take time for dating again.

Elvis' version of "Blue Christmas" was her favorite, so naturally, when it started playing around her, she had to clear her throat and join in. She glanced at the dash, at what was basically a computer screen—and they wondered why people had accidents on the road— to consult the GPS. Ten more miles and she would be in Amesbury. According to the time on the dash, she had plenty of time to get checked into the lodge and walk around the little ski town before her meeting.

She couldn't wait to see the place decked out for the holidays. Her brother, Christian, was the exact opposite. Hated snow, winter, Christmas—anything that wasn't stifling heat and sunshine and even soupy humidity. McKenzie used to wonder if she and Christian were adopted because they had such different ideas and interests. The question was ridiculous as she was a spitting image of her dad, and Christian of their mom. But she figured someday, when they were older and had their own families, she would be living somewhere with real seasons, leaves that changed colors in the fall, and white Christmases while Christian would be living somewhere beachy, where the only thing white about Christmas was the sand.

When she saw the billboard welcoming her to Amesbury— the pretty winter scene definitely made her feel cozy and welcome—she tapped her brakes with a glance in the rearview mirror. There was a car so far behind her she couldn't make out what it was, but other than that, nobody around. If she weren't the chipper, adventurous type that all her teachers had always noted on her report cards, she might find the lack of traffic, people, a little creepy. Instead, it only added to her hopes for a Hallmark-like atmosphere in this little Montana town.

McKenzie laughed at the thought of sending Snapchats to her brother. Hopefully, she would find cutesy, over-the-top holiday stuff to photograph like streetlights wrapped in silver garland and a Christmas tree farm with a hot chocolate stand draped with fairy lights and maybe even a Santa with rosy cheeks and a big belly. Oh yeah, if she saw anything of the kind while she was in Amesbury, she would unload on Christian! It would be a fun payback for the pictures he had sent from Miami last year. The joke was on him, though. McKenzie loved Christmas, but she didn't mind pictures of the ocean and the beach.

She signaled as she took the Amesbury exit, singing along with Otis Redding now to "Merry Christmas Baby." She couldn't sit still, so she was dancing in her seat with what she knew had to be a big, dopey grin on her face. Her first glance at the small town took her breath away.

Main Street was beautiful. Quaint little businesses lined both sides of the street—a mechanic's garage, restaurants, a coffee shop. McKenzie squealed softly as steered the SUV slowly down the street. She loved it here already. As soon as she got checked in at the lodge, she would text Lena and tell her about her first impressions of Amesbury.

CHAPTER TWO

D<small>URAN</small>

"Can you get that?"

Duran Carey glanced over his shoulder at his dad, ready to remind him that no, he couldn't answer the phone because he was up on a ladder getting something for a customer. But Gabriel, his dad, had his back to him, the handset of another phone pressed to his ear. With a quiet sigh, after all, this was their bread and butter and growling about being busy was not good form, Duran managed to wiggle the black puffer coat from the mannequin on the display shelf. Carefully, he backed down the fully extended ladder, coat in hand, and managed a sincere smile for the brunette who had stood at his feet worrying over him while he climbed.

"There you go."

"Thank you so much," she gushed. Duran nodded as he excused himself and hurried behind the counter to snatch up the still ringing phone.

"Don't do it, Stace."

He glanced at his dad, wondering what he was warning his mom not to do. No time to think about it right now, though. Not with seven customers browsing, four of them carrying items he hoped they planned to purchase, and the phone at his ear.

"Slopes." Duran watched a young kid eyeing a sled on the wall. "This is Duran. How can I help you?"

"I called earlier about ski rental."

"Yes, sir." Duran nodded. He had fielded more than one call about ski rental today, but he supposed announcing that to the caller would be rude.

"I think you reserved something for me. I need to cancel that," the caller told him. "My wife got sick."

"I'm sorry to hear that." Eyes on the computer screen now, Duran tapped at the keyboard. "What's the name?"

"Ginger and Allan Kerkhoff."

Duran typed the last name in, scanned the screen, and quickly found what he was looking for. The man had indeed reserved gear for tomorrow.

"Okay, Mr. Kerkhoff, I've canceled your reservation. Is there anything else I can do for you now?"

"No, thank you."

"You're welcome," Duran answered. "I hope your wife feels better."

"Thank you."

He hung up only to find his dad watching him through narrowed eyes.

"Whose wife is sick?"

"They rented ski stuff equipment for tomorrow. Called to cancel. What's going on with Mom?"

His dad rolled his eyes, but before he could even say don't ask, one of the customers who had been browsing for the better part of an hour appeared at the counter, her arms loaded down with merchandise.

"Did you take your lunch yet?"

"No." Duran scanned the store again, noting a customer near the front door. The guy had a boot box tucked under his arm. It wasn't often they had shoplifters or even attempted shoplifting. But it did happen occasionally. Still watching the customer, Duran spoke to his dad. "I can wait for a few minutes until we get things caught up here."

His dad offered the woman at the counter a big smile and a friendly greeting, but Duran saw the quick jerk of his gaze to the front door. He gave Duran a nearly imperceptible nod as he picked up the top item on the pile to scan it. Duran stepped up and started removing items from their hangers and folding them so he could scan and bag the items quicker. Gave him something to do while he covertly kept an eye on the guy with the boots.

"Where ya visiting from?" his dad asked the woman.

"Tennessee," she answered with a big smile.

"Nice." Dad nodded his approval. "Lived just outside of Chattanooga for a bit when I was a kid."

If Duran were younger, he might think his dad was blowing a line of pickle smoke at the woman. No matter where customers said they were from, his dad was familiar with their home, whether he'd lived there a while, knew someone who lived there, or had simply heard stories about a nearby town.

His dad was a consummate salesperson. As his mom liked to point out, Gabriel Carey was easy on the eyes, and surely, his looks drew a lot of women in and bade them stay longer. But his charm and his sincere knowledge and desire to help people didn't hurt, either.

"We're in the Gatlinburg area," the woman told him.

Duran felt a smile slide over his face as his dad did what he did best. Probably, he could have had the woman rung up and out the door in five minutes, but Gabe was in no hurry. While he was efficient, he still chatted as he worked, and even when the woman had tapped her credit card and put it away and held her bag in her hands, the two of them were still talking about Gatlinburg and Dollywood.

Excusing himself, Duran made the rounds of the store. The guy with the boots was back by shoes now, looking at socks. Duran made himself useful at a table of folded flannels. He refolded several and straightened the piles as his dad rung up three more customers, including the guy with the boots.

Finally, they were alone in the store. It wouldn't last long. Slopes Outdoor Gear did a solid business all year long, but things got crazy during the holidays. Duran figured a lot of people traveled here for conferences and vacations. Maybe they under packed and needed things for themselves or maybe they liked the idea of buying Christmas gifts from an outdoorsy store in a mountain town. Maybe both.

Whatever the case, Duran knew they had precious seconds before the doors opened and someone else wandered in.

"What's going on with Mom?" he asked now.

"Nancy Vahle fell on the ice last night."

"What ice?" Duran asked with a frown. They'd had some snow, but there hadn't been any ice storm around here yet this year.

"On their driveway." Dad shrugged. "I dunno. Something about Harold and the garden hose. Long story short, she broke her hip."

Duran stared at his dad with wide eyes. "Oh, no."

"Yeah, oh no."

"Mom volunteered again, didn't she?"

The last time something like this happened, the seventh-grade teacher at St. Anne's had landed in the hospital with meningitis just before the school science fair. And even though Duran's parents had a trip to Niagara Falls planned, his mom had ended up volunteering to help. His dad had canceled the trip, but if Duran remembered correctly, the two had done the whole fight and silent treatment gamut before finally making up.

Duran wasn't sure, but this almost sounded like it could be worse. His parents were supposed to be leaving soon for an anniversary cruise. Nancy Vahle was the kindergarten teacher. The one in charge of the annual Christmas program.

"I'm goin' to lunch," Duran announced. If his dad was anywhere near blowing up, he was ready to escape it for now. And maybe by the time Duran came back, his dad would be over it.

Doubtful, though. Because his mom was the most selfless person he knew, and odds were, she had already taken up the job of running the program.

CHAPTER THREE

"But did you see Santa?"

McKenzie laughed softly as she tugged her suitcase into her room. Unable to wait to gush to Lena about how picturesque Amesbury was, she had called her supervisor the minute she walked away from the reception desk at the lodge. Naturally, the call had dropped the second the elevator doors closed on her, but McKenzie had called her back as soon as she was on her floor. She had filled Lena in on the perfect blanket of snow covering the ground, how charming Main Street was, and the garland wrapped around every streetlight she had seen as she approached the lodge—eight; she'd counted them as she drove.

"Well, no. Not yet," she answered as her door closed behind her. She eyed her room with excitement. The buffalo plaid comforter looked cozy and warm. The chunky wooden bed frame and chairs by the fireplace were rugged looking but inviting. "But I'm going back out in a few minutes, so who knows? Maybe I'll find him."

"Send pictures if you do," Lena said with a laugh.

"Oh, I will."

"What's the lodge look like?"

McKenzie let go of her luggage and crossed the room to stand at the window. She surveyed Main Street, the same street she'd just driven down. Feeling like a little girl, she couldn't wait for evening to come, so she could see Amesbury lit up.

"It's nice," she answered. "Looks on the newish side. My room's great."

"Good."

"I'll check back in with you later," McKenzie told her.

Knowing she should call her mom, too, McKenzie tossed her phone on the bed and went back to the door to grab her suitcase. Wheeling it over to the closet, she found the luggage rack and plopped her suitcase on it. She'd seen a coffee shop, so calling her mom could wait a few minutes. She would hang her clothes first, and then grab her phone and head down Main to get coffee. Odds were, the place would be cozy and warm, so she would sit there for a bit and talk to her mom.

After hanging her blouses in the closet and putting her toiletries and cosmetics in the bathroom, McKenzie snatched her phone up from the bed. She sent her mom a quick text to let her know she'd made it to Amesbury and was checked into her hotel and promised to call in a few minutes. Making sure she had her key card tucked in her slim card case, she turned the bedside lamp on and then headed out.

She stopped several times on her walk to the coffee shop to take pictures of the cute little town all decked out for Christmas. Imagining Christian's cringe when he opened it, McKenzie laughed as she sent a Snapchat of the painted front window of a toy store. Not the real Santa yet, but she loved the jolly-looking Santa pictured there. She passed a fancy Italian restaurant. The garlicky aroma made her belly rumble, reminding her she hadn't eaten since before her flight. But The Hideaway Restaurant looked inviting, too. She imagined a plate with hot mashed potatoes and gravy later this evening, maybe a pot roast special or even meatloaf.

As she walked by The Sweet Tooth, she slowed her steps. No doubt she and Christian shared this gene from their dad. She eyed the colorful candies as she passed and made a mental note to stop in before heading home. The continuous buzzing of her phone drew her attention away from the candy store, so she answered her phone as she continued walking.

"Hello?"

Even bundled up in her bright red puffer coat, she shivered as she walked down the block. The coffee shop was coming up; she was sure of it.

"Could I speak with McKenzie Noble, please?"

"This is she," she answered, a smile crossing her face when she saw two older ladies ringing bells at a Salvation Army red bucket in front of what appeared to be a fresh food market. One of them was singing "Here Comes Santa Claus" while the other appeared ready to dig a hole and crawl in. McKenzie stuck her free hand in her coat pocket and pulled out a few wrinkled ones and thirty-two cents in change.

"Bless you," the woman who wasn't singing called after her as she walked.

Charming and cute, McKenzie wished she had taken a picture of the ladies as she walked away. Then again, they might consider her a rude, big-city girl if she did that. She wasn't either of the above, but she was a newcomer here in Amesbury, so she wanted to be pleasant and polite.

"Hi, McKenzie, this is Jarrett Hunt from the Sterling Lodge. We were supposed to meet this afternoon?"

Worried she had misjudged how much time she had or worse—noted the time of their meeting wrong in her schedule—she fought down a flash of panic.

"Yes?" She cleared her throat when she heard how uncertain she sounded.

"I'm so sorry, but something's come up. I have a bit of a family emergency. Could we possibly reschedule for tomorrow?"

Again, she slowed her walk, but this time because she was concerned about this guy's family emergency.

"Absolutely," she answered. "I'm so sorry."

"My mother-in-law had an accident," he told her. "My wife is with her. I need to get my kids from—"

"It's no trouble," she interrupted him.

"Okay. This is ridiculous, but do you mind if we wait until tomorrow morning to reschedule? I need to see what exactly's going on and make sure I get my kids to school—"

"I don't mind at all," she promised him. Maybe a more seasoned businesswoman would wonder why Jarrett Hunt didn't have someone else who could meet with her. But she wasn't in any hurry to wrap things up and get out of town. In fact, at Lena's urging, she had taken the rest of the week to hang out here in Amesbury for a mini vacation. She had been a bit uncertain at first; she didn't usually travel alone.

Maybe watching all those Hallmark Christmas movies had pushed her to take Lena's suggestion. Whatever had made her change her mind, now that she was here, she was glad she would be staying a few days. Plenty of time to soak up the festive holiday culture.

Starting now since she no longer had anything on her plate the rest of the day.

"Thank you so much. I'll call you as soon as I have an idea what's going on in the morning."

"Thanks for calling," she answered and then added, "And good luck with the emergency. I hope everything is okay."

"Thanks."

She hated to be happy about a change in plans due to any sort of emergency, but she certainly wasn't upset at the idea of exploring the small town now rather than waiting until tomorrow.

The sign for the coffee shop she had noticed earlier came into view. Realizing now that there was a cute little pile of books on the sign and noticing as she got closer that the windows here were painted with a Christmas scene complete with a tree and books with bows on them, McKenzie felt again like a little kid at the North Pole.

She was about to step inside a coffee shop and bookstore in a cute little Christmas town, and there was no one around to tap his or her foot waiting on her to finish browsing and leave. Because coffee and books had always been her happy place, she snapped another picture and sent it to Christian, chuckling to herself as she imagined the way he would roll his eyes when he opened it.

CHAPTER FOUR

DURAN

Most days, Duran brought his lunch with him to work—whether it was something left over from The Hideout Restaurant or from whatever sketchy sort of dinner he had thrown together for himself the night before. He didn't love spending money on takeout food every day, not when there was usually something good at home he could take. But the new Ford Bishop book came out today, so he'd planned to grab a burger to go at The Hideout and pack it back to Caffeinated Bliss where he could buy his copy and sit down to read a chapter or two while he ate.

With his phone in his pocket and the ringer on in case his dad got busy and needed a hand, Duran pulled his black coat on and headed out the door. The snow had already stopped. He looked up and down the block as he walked to the restaurant, trying to decide if the snow that had fallen today had amounted to anything. Judging from the mostly clear streets and the thin layer of white over the cars currently parked in the area, he decided it hadn't.

The Amesbury Chamber of Commerce had installed speakers up and down Main Street a few years back, so Christmas music surrounded him as he walked. Most of the guys he had gone to school with here in Amesbury hated it, couldn't get out of town fast enough. Duran had left for college, but he had been happy to return with his business degree in hand to help his dad with the family store.

While Duran stayed in contact with a few of his friends from high school, the boys he had grown up with here in Amesbury, he knew most of them hated the cliché town. The over-the-top holiday festivities. He didn't find fault with them any more than they dissed him for his love of all things Christmas.

Not even Willie Nelson's twangy, nasally voice singing "Frosty the Snowman" bothered him. In fact, he liked it. Hands in his pockets, he hummed along as he approached The Hideout Restaurant. Seeing Linda Kendrick across the street, he lifted a hand in greeting as he pulled the door of the restaurant open. Linda and her sister Wanda volunteered to ring the bells for the Salvation Army buckets every year; Wanda fancied herself a singer. Linda always seemed traumatized, but she was always willing to volunteer the following year. Duran got a kick out of wondering where exactly they would pop up each year.

No wonder Linda was smiling like the Cheshire cat; where was Wanda today? Most likely, she had ducked inside to warm up a bit.

A wall of heat rolled over him as he stepped inside The Hideout Restaurant. As usual, the place was hopping, even if it was late afternoon, the lunch hour long gone. Every stool that lined the counter was taken by the same older men who passed every afternoon here. Inside, Brenda Lee sang "Rockin' Around the Christmas Tree." Duran nodded a greeting at the group before turning to the new woman at the register.

"To go order for Carey."

She nodded as she grabbed the brown paper bag.

"Got it right here, Mr. Carey."

"Duran, please," he told her with a smile.

"Peggy." She took the cash he offered her and tossed the coins in a collection jar when he waved off his change. Currently, the money collected in the jar would be used toward toys for kids whose families were struggling, but Duran knew it changed from season to season and year to year.

"Nice to meet you, Peggy." He grabbed the bag, stomach growling at the delicious smells of the burger and fries. "Enjoy the rest of your day."

"Thank you."

As he stepped outside, he left Brenda Lee behind and walked back toward Caffeinated Bliss singing along with Johnny Mathis' version of "Winter Wonderland." He waved and nodded at almost everyone—another thing about life in Amesbury that his friends, well *most people his age* didn't like. Amesbury was a small town; everyone knew everyone. And yes, very cliché, but everyone knew everyone's business.

Funny. Duran didn't mind it. Maybe if his family had been through a big trauma, he would find it annoying. There were times when well-meaning townsfolk had nearly smothered him with their questions and concern when he and Kaeli broke up. They had dated all through high school, so naturally, the entire Amesbury population had assumed they would get married and start a family. Duran had kind of assumed the same thing, though he knew there would be a little lag time in there. Kaeli had wanted to go to medical school since she was in sixth grade, so he knew they wouldn't get married right away.

But Kaeli had blown his mind, along with everyone else in Amesbury's minds, when she gave him his class ring back before they left for college. Duran had studied in Denver. Kaeli had chosen Boston, and as far as he knew, she had never looked back. He hadn't seen her or talked to her since she left.

Caffeinated Bliss was busy, too. Amesbury was a thriving little town, but business was always a little bit better in the winter, especially during the holiday season. Though it was small, it was an affluent town, with tourists here to enjoy the adventurous outdoors.

"Duran." The manager waved at him when he pulled the door open, and the bell above his head jingled. "How ya doing?"

"Hey, Tom." Duran nodded. "Busy today. You guys?"

"Steady," the man answered. "You're here for the Ford Bishop book."

"I am. Gonna grab a table and read a chapter or two over lunch."

"Good plan." Tom turned to grab the book off the back counter and scanned it. Duran hurried over to the only open table in the place and put his bagged lunch down. He unzipped his coat, shrugged it off, and hooked it on his chair before going back to the counter to pay for the book. Because this was his habit, Tom already had an iced tea waiting for him by the register, too.

In here, a soft jazzy instrumental version of "Sleigh Ride" played. Perfect for reading. Duran didn't trust himself not to sing along if anyone else was singing. He carried his book and drink to the table, nodding at a few familiar faces.

A blond woman sat at the last two-top table in the seating area. Legs crossed, she had one hand curled around one of the chunky Caffeinated Bliss mug, and she held an open hardback book in her other hand. She looked up suddenly, catching Duran watching her. He stubbed his toe on his chair as their eyes locked.

Hers were a soft, cornflower blue, fringed with thick dark lashes. Her cheekbones were sharp, but her smile was soft and sweet. She wasn't from around here; he would know. No question she was a tourist, but Duran wondered if she was visiting Amesbury alone.

"It's good." She nodded and pointed at the book in his hand. Duran glanced at the Ford Bishop book and then back at her, only for her to close the book in her hand and show him the front.

"You're a Ford Bishop fan?" he asked with a grin.

"Of course, I am."

CHAPTER FIVE

"Have you read the whole series?"

McKenzie cocked her head and sighed at the fellow Ford Bishop reader.

"How could I *not* read the whole series?" She shook her head as if she was disappointed in him. The guy—and yes, he was every bit as good-looking as an actor out of a Hallmark movie—laughed softly as he straddled the chair backwards to look at her rather than his table.

"A lot of people didn't like *Hell Storm*." He shrugged as he draped his arms over the back of the chair, fingers wrapped around the book.

"I didn't love *Hell Storm*, but I read it," she answered simply.

Judging from the fact that the guy was dressed in black Cons, jeans, and a red thermal shirt, as well as the fact that he'd brought a brown bag in with him, which McKenzie assumed was lunch, she figured he was a local. It was possible he was her age, give or take a year or two. A few dark curls escaped from under his black beanie and fell in a riot over his thick dark brows.

"I don't understand the hate for it." He chewed on his lower lip for a second as if lost in thought.

"It was just kind of weak," she told him. "Almost the same plot as book three, and even then, it was kind of watered down."

"I guess." He nodded.

"Is that your lunch?" she asked.

"Late lunch. Early supper." He shrugged.

"You better eat it while it's hot."

"Join me?" he offered.

McKenzie blinked at him. Was he offering her half of his lunch? She almost laughed at the thought. She wouldn't take his food, but she would need to find something to eat soon. When she'd first come into the coffee shop, she had been thrilled to see the new Ford Bishop book. And then she'd been overwhelmed by the delicious aromas of coffee and baked treats. So while she talked to her mom on the phone, she had devoured a lemon cupcake. And she was still drinking her coffee.

Plenty of sugar and caffeine. Things could get ugly fast.

Maybe he just wanted to talk about books. Whatever the case, McKenzie liked the idea of talking to the guy for a while, so she climbed to her feet and packed her belongings up. She tucked her coat and book under one arm, and then picked up her phone and coffee to carry it over to his table.

The guy sprang off his chair like a Jack-in-the-Box when she neared him.

"Here. Let me." He held his hand out to help her, so she turned just enough for him to take the book and her coat from under her elbow. "I'm Duran."

He hooked her coat over the back of the other chair at the table.

"McKenzie," she answered as she sat down.

"Which one's your favorite?"

"The first one." She fired her answer back without pausing to think.

"No way." He shook his head as he stacked their books and set them aside. McKenzie approved of the precaution. A book lover would not want his or her book to get ketchup or mustard or iced tea on the cover or even a page. "Book five."

"Because Arkin died?" she asked quietly. "You didn't like him?"

She might have to reconsider moving to this guy's table. Arkin Lemaster was one of her favorite characters in the series.

"No, I loved him. And it gutted me when he died." Duran pulled a burger wrapped in wax paper from the bag. McKenzie hoped he didn't hear her stomach rumble. "But the emotional stakes in that book were through the roof. And the writing was phenomenal."

He was right.

She picked up her coffee for a drink and then pursed her lips to stare at him for a moment.

"You disagree?" he finally asked after he had swallowed a couple of bites of his sandwich.

"No, actually, you're right."

Putting the burger down, he wiped his hands on a napkin and took a drink.

"Why do you think the first one is the best?"

"Because it's all new. I love the first book in any series I read. It's the reader's introduction to a whole new world."

"True." He nodded. "Are you here on vacation? Ski trip?"

McKenzie put her cup down and shook her head, easily following the change in conversation.

"No, actually, I'm here for work."

"Hmm." Duran narrowed his eyes at her as he pulled a small order of fries from his bag. "You don't look like a ski instructor."

Her laugh surprised her, but she leaned sideways to take in her jeans and long brown boots.

"I don't?"

He flashed a grin at her. "What do you do?"

"I work for Inovial Educational Consulting. We develop textbooks and tech for current curriculum."

"And you're in Amesbury for that?" Duran tipped his head.

"Well, I'm here to meet with the manager at Sterling Lodge. IEC is looking to hold a conference here in Amesbury. I'm here to scout out the area and talk to the manager. Look at prices for room blocks and conference rooms in the winter versus the off-season."

"Hmm." He nodded and took another bite of his burger. "That's interesting."

"I was supposed to meet with the manager today, but he called and said he had a bit of a family emergency."

"Mm." Duran took a drink of his tea before he spoke. "Yep. His mother-in-law fell and broke her hip."

"How do you know that?"

"Small town," he answered. "And my mom is the school secretary where Mrs. Vahle teaches."

"And Mrs. Vahle is his mother-in-law?"

"Yep." Duran chuckled softly. "Not laughing at Mrs. Vahle. She's a very nice person. But accidents have a way of causing all sorts of ripple effects."

"True."

He glanced at his phone and wolfed down the rest of his burger. "Speaking of which, I should get back to work."

"I'm on page fifty-two," she told him.

"Already?"

McKenzie looked up at him when he stood and gathered his trash.

"I mean, it's good." She shrugged.

"How long are you in town?"

"The rest of the week," she answered.

"Are you meeting with the lodge manager every day?" he asked with a frown.

"Oh, gosh no. My boss strongly encouraged me to spend a few days here and soak up the Christmas scenes."

"A mini vacation."

"Yeah, kind of."

"Good." He flashed her a big smile. "Maybe we can discuss the book when we're finished reading it."

"I'd like that," she answered with a nod.

It occurred to her as he threw his stuff away and walked out the door, still pulling his coat on, that they hadn't exchanged contact information in order to get together to talk about the book or anything else.

Then again, as McKenzie had just learned, Amesbury was a small town, and she and Duran were bound to run into each other again.

Anything else?

McKenzie snorted to herself. She had definitely watched too many Hallmark movies if she was thinking she and Duran would get together to do anything other than discuss the Ford Bishop book. She decided to keep those thoughts to herself; no sense in handing Lena or anyone in her family ammunition they could use to tease her.

CHAPTER SIX

His parents were still arguing via phone call when he went back to work. The only thing different that Duran could see was that maybe the fight had escalated a bit. Rather than stick around the front counter and listen to his dad's side of the phone call, Duran looked for something to do as far from his dad as possible.

Which meant he spent most of the second part of his shift in the stockroom, only going up front when he heard the bells over the door ring. As far as their argument went, Duran understood his dad's frustration. His parents had an anniversary trip planned, and they deserved to take the time off and enjoy themselves. He knew without even listening to the conversation that his dad was reminding his mom that there were plenty of other faculty members at the school who could take over the Christmas program.

And Duran agreed with him.

But on the other hand, Duran knew his mom better than to think she would leave town on vacation not knowing for certain that the program was in good hands. Stacey Carey loved Christmas, and she loved spreading Christmas cheer. The fact that the little kids, their families, and even the community at large enjoyed the program would weigh heavily on her.

He was exhausted by the time his dad flipped the closed sign on the door, more so from avoiding his dad than the actual work involved in running the store. Once his dad had the register balanced and the bank deposit ready, Duran urged him on out into the cold with a promise that he would have the store straightened and in tip top shape for tomorrow.

With the store quiet, he moved quickly through the process of straightening the rows and rows of folded clothing items, setting all the shoes and boots on display back to the correct angle, and organizing all the hanging clothing by sizes. Once that was done, he swept the floor and then locked up to head home.

New book tucked under his arm, Duran hunched his shoulders in his coat as he walked through the brisk cold to the parking lot behind the store. At his truck, though, he hesitated and looked back toward the building. He had been in a hurry to get home and scrounge for some leftovers to eat while he started reading. Now, though, he wondered about McKenzie, fellow Ford Bishop fan and maybe his new reader friend.

What was she doing tonight? He cursed himself for not thinking to get her contact information. On the other hand, Amesbury was small enough that unless she high tailed it out of town the second he had walked away from Caffeinated Bliss, she wasn't much more than a stone's throw in any direction away from him.

Before he could change his mind, he unlocked his door and put the book on his seat. He dropped his head back to look at the star-lined sky as he swung the door closed again. Heading back toward the store, he aimed his key fob over his shoulder, satisfied when he heard the beep of the lock.

Hands tucked in his pockets, he walked the long way around Slopes and then wandered down Main Street. Most of the shops and offices were closed by now. In the off-season, most of Main Street was shut down by five. During the holiday season, the closing hour changed to seven, and there were a few rogue places that stayed open until nine.

Duran found himself humming along to the Christmas music playing as he walked. The speakers along the main drag were well-hidden; the store fronts and offices along Main Street were all tastefully decorated. No exposed wires or speakers to ruin the mood. He heard a low buzz of conversation as he neared Whitby's Tree Farm Stand. With a smile on his face and his hands still in his pockets, he slowed at the rustic wooden sign for the tree market. A few couples stood with Kenny Whitby, the old man who owned the tree farm. Duran nodded at him when Kenny looked his way.

The trees had already been picked over, but from where Duran stood, he could see some nice looking smaller Blue Spruces. He saw a flash of blond hair and a bright red coat, so he slipped by the small group talking to Kenny and made his way to where McKenzie stood admiring a good-sized fir tree.

"Fancy meeting you here," he said by way of greeting.

McKenzie flashed him a grin over her shoulder. "Hey. Are you looking for a tree?"

"Nope. I was actually looking for you."

"Me?" She turned to him, her front teeth nibbling on her lower lip. Duran loved the sparkle in her eyes and her rosy, pink cheeks. How long had she been outside?

"Yeah." He shrugged. "Just wondering how the book is."

She laughed softly and ducked her head.

"Did you finish it?"

"No!" She looked up again and shook her head. "No. Are you kidding me? I feel like I'm at the North Pole. I'm trying to soak it all in."

"Did you get some hot chocolate?" Duran nodded his head toward the back of the tree market where the Whitbys always set up a card table and a big thermos filled with hot cocoa.

"I already had coffee and a pastry earlier. And I might have ducked into that little candy store." Her already rosy cheeks flushed pink with embarrassment, but Duran only laughed. "You'll find hot cocoa and holiday treats pretty much everywhere you go in Amesbury right now."

"Yeah?" She shoved her hands in her coat pockets. "Is it the same where you work?"

"Mm-hmm."

"How do you stay so skinny?"

"I am not skinny," he protested. "Svelte, maybe. Fit. But not skinny."

McKenzie snorted and stomped her feet a couple of times. Duran knew the move well; she was cold, trying to get some feeling back in her numbed toes.

"Where do you work?' she asked him now.

"Slopes."

"On the slopes?" She tipped her head. "Like what? You're a ski instructor?"

"No. My dad owns an outdoor gear and clothing store called Slopes."

"Oh." She flashed him a grin and looked around, as if searching for the store. "That sounds fun."

"It can be," he agreed.

"Do you ski?"

"I do," he nodded, "but maybe not well enough to be an instructor."

"I tried it once a few years ago. Just out of college."

"How'd it go?"

"Let's just say I've never been in a hurry to try it again."

"How about a walking tour of Amesbury?" he suggested. "Although I guess you've probably already seen most of Main Street."

"I'd like that," she told him.

"Did you pet the reindeer yet?"

McKenzie looked up at him as they walked side by side back through the entrance to the tree market.

"Are you kidding?"

"I'm not." He drew a cross over his heart. "Cross my heart."

"Well, if you're crossing your heart, it must be true. I'd love to see the reindeer."

CHAPTER SEVEN

McKenzie

She wasn't sure if she should believe him, but McKenzie walked willingly with Duran as he headed north on Main Street. He fished a bit as they walked, trying to get her to spill something about the book they were both reading. She wouldn't give him any hints about the storyline; as much as he wanted to know what was going on in the book, she knew he wanted to read it for himself. She would be the same if the roles were reversed.

"Ohmygosh." She laughed out loud when they neared the small penned-in area where there were indeed two reindeer roaming.

"You didn't believe me."

The mock hurt tone and the dramatic way he put his hand over his heart made her laugh again.

"I was skeptical," she admitted. "They're beautiful."

"They are pretty neat," he agreed. "C'mon. You can pet them."

"Are they mean?"

"Would Santa fly with animals that are mean?"

Duran reached for her. Without a second thought, McKenzie pulled her hand from her pocket and linked her gloved fingers with his.

"So, these guys are the actual reindeer on loan from Santa, huh?"

"Nah. They're all pretty busy this time of year," he told her as he led her right up to the wooden fence. "These guys are relatives."

As they stood at the fence, the smaller of the reindeer approached them cautiously. McKenzie gasped softly when Duran gently stroked the animal's snout. She looked up at Duran and then turned her attention back to the reindeer. The animal was beautiful. She hadn't seen a lot of reindeer in her life—only those in the Christmas movies she had watched as a kid—but these two looked healthy and well cared for.

While McKenzie liked animals and had volunteered at the shelter back at home often, her brother was a stickler about animal rights. She wanted to send him a snapchat of the reindeer, but she was aware that he wouldn't approve of them being penned in here solely for display purposes.

"Where are they from?" she asked Duran now. Maybe if she could assure Christian the animals were cared for, she would send him a picture.

"Well, we were just at the tree market, right? Whitby's Tree Farm does the tree market every year. And then Kenny Whitby's brother-in-law, Judd Hoover, has a big farm a few miles down the road where he raises the reindeer. He's got other livestock, too."

McKenzie flinched at the mention of other livestock. When the reindeer leaned forward over the fence, she rubbed her fingertips over his nose.

"We should have brought treats."

"Like what? Carrots?"

"Did you leave carrots out for Rudolph when you were a kid?" Duran aimed an amused grin at her.

McKenzie gave herself a mental shake. The guy's smile was dazzling; out here in this romantic, festive atmosphere, it was dangerous.

"I might have," she admitted quietly. "Until I was seven and saw my mom nibbling on the carrots my brother and I left out for Rudolph."

"She ate the carrots? I think I'd go for Santa's cookies."

"My dad ate those," she answered with a laugh.

"These guys like apples for treats." Thankfully, he shifted his warm brown eyes back to the reindeer. McKenzie felt like she could breathe again, now that Duran wasn't pinning her in place with that intense stare. "And raisins."

"Raisins?"

"Yep. I've seen Judd give them raisins for treats."

"Wow." She arched her eyebrows thoughtfully as she studied the reindeer again. The animal wore a deep red collar with the name *Barry* embroidered in gold stitching. "Barry," she tried the name out and decided that even though it wouldn't be her first choice of a name for a reindeer, it fit him. In fact, the animal seemed to cock his head at her when she spoke his name.

"Manilow."

"What?" Hand still hanging over the fence, she looked up at Duran with wide eyes.

"His name. Barry Manilow."

"Seriously?"

While she stared at Duran, the other reindeer—this one much taller, his antlers much bigger—meandered over and dipped his nose under her hand. She laughed as she tore her gaze away from Duran to look at the reindeer. They certainly were domesticated. Still, her brother's voice echoed in her head; they were wild animals, and they should be free to roam the land. Not cooped up on some reindeer farm or penned in a small area for some small-town holiday festivities.

"Oh wow." She snorted when she saw the second reindeer's collar. "Elvis Presley, right?"

"Yep." Duran sounded amused; she wondered if it was the reindeer or her reaction to them that he was enjoying. "They have a horse named Wayne Newton and a dog named Casey Kasem, too."

"They must be interesting people."

"Amesbury is an interesting town," he said with a shrug. "The family that runs the outdoor gear and clothing shop is really fun."

"You've heard that, huh?"

"Well, they usually are." His smile shifted a bit, and for a second, McKenzie thought he looked uncomfortable. Maybe even unhappy. "Gimme your phone."

"What?" She frowned up at him, but she was already reaching to pull her phone from her pocket.

"I'll take your picture," he told her. "Got any nieces or nephews? I'm sure they'd get a kick out of seeing you with reindeer." McKenzie handed her phone over to him. "You can send them a picture with Santa later, too. Remind them Santa's always watching."

"Santa's here?" McKenzie looked over her shoulder. The street was all lit up for the holiday, and tinny Christmas music reached them from the last of the stores along Main Street. But she didn't see Santa Claus or his house.

"Of course," Duran said sternly. "Hold still."

McKenzie snorted softly as she looked up at Duran. He tapped her phone a few times, studied the pictures with a goofy smile, and finally gave her phone back to her. She looked at the pictures quickly, pleased with them but wanting more.

"You get in here, too," she suggested.

"Me?" Duran sounded delighted.

"Yeah. Let's do a selfie."

"Okay." He moved to stand beside her and took her phone again, since his arms were longer. McKenzie looked up with a smile, but she wasn't thinking about reindeer or Santa. She didn't have nieces or nephews. Nope, the smile was about her friends. What they would say when they saw pictures of her in this Christmas town with this movie star good-looking guy.

Again, Duran took a few pictures, both of them smiling, bookended by the reindeer—also looking up as if aware they were in a picture.

"You didn't answer me." He turned to her when he dropped his hand to his side.

"No nieces or nephews." She shook her head. "But I could always threaten my brother with Santa pictures."

"How old is he?"

"Twenty-two."

"Does he like reindeer?"

She flinched again and shrugged. "Sure. But not reindeer penned up for us to gawk at."

"Oh. Guess he's not much into zoos, then?"

McKenzie laughed. "Nope. He's not."

"We could go out to Judd's farm," he suggested. "It's a great place. Big, open spaces for the animals to roam, and they're well cared for."

"I'd love that."

The words slipped out before she realized she was going to speak. She considered scrambling to take them back or saying something silly to make light of what she'd just said. But the look on Duran's face stopped her. He seemed excited about taking her there.

"Perfect." He nodded. "We'll do that in daylight so you can see the area better. Actually, we should go in late afternoon as dusk settles. The whole place is done up for Christmas."

"Oh." She arched her brows, not sure how it could be better than Main Street here in Amesbury. But she definitely wanted to see it now.

"For now, let's go find Santa's house."

She swallowed hard and looked around. "I'm not ready to see Santa."

"Yeah?" Duran quirked an eyebrow at her as he scrubbed each of the reindeer on their heads again. McKenzie saw him nod at the young guy across the pen, apparently the reindeer handler for the evening. "Have you been a bad girl?"

She chuckled. "Not bad, bad. But, Santa's a big deal."

"He is." Duran nodded. "It's okay. He won't be there now, but we can still see his house."

"And you'll take me back when Santa is there?"

"Sure." There was that dangerous smile again. "You gonna go back to your room and get right with the big guy before you talk to Mr. Claus?"

"Maybe."

His laughter sounded a bit wicked; McKenzie shivered as they walked.

"Cold?"

Of course he noticed. She looked up to meet his eyes, nodded, and chalked up another lie on her list of bad girl things.

CHAPTER EIGHT

DURAN

"So, you've lived here all your life?"

Duran glanced at McKenzie as they walked back down Main Street toward Santa's house.

"Left for college," he answered with a nod. "Most of my friends never came back after school."

"But you love it here." She looked up at him and tipped her head in askance.

"I do." He nodded. "Close to my family, too."

"Do you have siblings?"

"No. Just me and my parents."

Duran didn't want to think about his parents right now. They would be home from work; they'd be finished with dinner. But were they arguing? Would his mom insist on canceling the trip to make sure the Christmas program went off without a hitch?

"That's nice."

Gene Autry serenaded them now as they headed to Santa's house.

"Why isn't Santa's house close to the reindeer?"

He laughed softly. "It used to be. But little kids get a little rambunctious. Some little kids are afraid of Santa. Some just get tired and grouchy when they have to stand around and wait in lines. The noise kind of bothered the reindeer."

"Hmm." She nodded as she considered his answer. "I guess that makes sense."

"That's it up there."

Santa's little cottage was straight ahead, a block away. The cottage itself was small and unassuming, but the small yard around it was loaded with decorations. Life sized elves and snowmen crowded the area. Lights shaped like lollipops lined the walkway to the bright red door, which was currently closed. A tall black lantern lit the whole block; a wooden sign hanging from the lantern proclaiming it Santa's Village.

"Wow." McKenzie took it all in with wide eyes and a smile of wonder on her face. "It's beautiful."

"I like it, too," he agreed.

He did like it. Duran loved seeing little kids all wide-eyed and excited watching Santa and his elves at the house. That part of him understood his mom's need to make sure the program would still happen.

"I can't imagine being a little kid and coming here to sit on Santa's lap." When she looked at Duran, her eyes sparkled with excitement.

Or holiday magic.

The thought almost made him laugh out loud. Duran was well aware he lived in the perfect setting for a Christmas movie. And his mom watched enough Hallmark movies that he knew how they worked.

Big city guy or girl visited a small town during the holidays. Met the small-town hero or heroine in some crazy cute catastrophe moment. They spent time together; did all the festive things. Fell in love. But refused to admit it, until it came time for the big city person to leave the small town.

He had no idea where McKenzie was from. And she didn't quite fit the cookie cutter mold for the big city character. She obviously loved Christmas. She wasn't complaining about the cold or Santa or reindeer poop on Main Street.

Duran wasn't looking to fall in love with her, either. Someday, he supposed he wanted to settle down with the right person. Have a family. But right now, he liked his bachelor life. His little townhouse rental just off Main. His job. No need to make any dramatic changes.

He loved McKenzie's smile, though.

And her laugh—in defiance of the Christmas movie clichés, it didn't sound like twinkling sleigh bells. She had a good, hearty laugh that made him happy.

Oh boy.

Time to move on.

"We'll come again tomorrow," he announced. "After your meeting."

She flashed a bright smile at him and nodded. "Sounds good."

"What's on your Christmas list?"

"Hmm?"

"What're you gonna ask him for tomorrow?"

That laugh again. Duran felt his smile grow, despite the little talking-to he had just given himself.

"Oh, no. I just want to see him. No need to talk to him."

"Nope." Duran shook his head. "You have to talk to him. Get your picture with him."

She locked her gaze with his as they walked. "Seriously?"

"Yep. It's part of the Amesbury charm. The whole Christmas experience. You don't want to miss out on that, do you?"

She nibbled on her lip and finally shook her head. "No, I don't wanna miss out on that."

"Good."

"Where are we going?"

"I thought I'd walk you back to the lodge."

"You don't have to do that." She shook her head.

"No, I don't. The crime rate's pretty low here. Not sure anything's happened at the police station since Marvin got loose and ate Mrs. Konrath's ham last Easter."

"Who's Marvin?" She arched an eyebrow. A tiny smile played at her lips. "Do I want to know?"

"Marvin is Don Kirkpatrick's German shepherd. Mrs. Konrath hates animals. It's like Marvin knows it, so he constantly picks on her."

"Picks on her?"

"Just ornery things. He wouldn't hurt a fly. Unless that fly or anything else was threatening Don or his family."

"And Mrs. Konrath called the police?"

"She did."

"What did they do?"

"Put Marv in the slammer. What else?"

McKenzie narrowed her eyes at him. "Seriously?'

"Yeah. He did an hour, at least. Slept off the food coma before Don busted him loose."

"I wanna meet Marvin."

"We can absolutely do that," he agreed with an enthusiastic nod.

"We can?"

"You don't believe me again, do you?"

"It sounds a little Mayberry to me."

"I'll take you to meet Marvin. And I'll show you his jail cell."

"Okay."

The music faded as they left Main Street and headed up the entry way to the Sterling Lodge. Duran stepped around her to push the door open for her and then followed her inside.

"This was fun," she told him. "Thank you."

"It was fun," he agreed. "Come find me. After your interview. If you wanna see more of Amesbury."

"Oh, I do." She nodded before he even finished speaking. "Put your number in my phone."

Duran took her phone and tapped his number in under new contacts. He put his full name in, ignoring that little niggling feeling that they were simply actors playing parts in a cheesy Christmas movie.

She smiled up at him when he handed her phone back to her. Their fingers brushed, but she was wearing gloves, so there was no zing of attraction or chemistry. Then again, Duran wasn't sure he needed it to know he was attracted to McKenzie.

One look at Caffeinated Bliss had been enough for him to know that.

"Goodnight, McKenzie."

"Goodnight."

CHAPTER NINE

MᴄKᴇɴᴢɪᴇ

Maybe it was the festive walk around Amesbury with Duran, or maybe it was simply the early morning for traveling, but McKenzie slept well. She often awoke remembering crazy dreams, but her first morning in Amesbury, she awoke feeling refreshed, with no memory of dreams or tossing and turning.

She'd texted her mom when she got in after wandering around with Duran, but not to share anything about him. Her mom might read too much into that, and her dad might load up her brother so the two of them could chase Duran down and interrogate him. McKenzie had simply told her mom that she'd been out exploring the cute little town, and she was back in her room for the night.

Ready for another fun day, she climbed out of bed and carried her phone with her to the bathroom. She found a Christmas playlist on her music streaming app and let it play while she showered and brushed her teeth. Wondering when she would hear from the manager at the lodge, she eyed the phone screen as she dabbed a bit of blush on her cheeks and swiped mascara over her lashes.

When she was finished in the bathroom, she tidied up the bed and folded the clothes she'd taken off last night. Rather than sit in her room to wait for a call, she grabbed her backpack and headed downstairs to the lobby. The scent of coffee hung in the air. She might have followed her nose to the coffee pot, but the giant tree in front of the huge bay windows at the back of the lobby, decorated for Christmas, caught her eyes. Coffee could wait a minute, she decided as she took a couple of pictures of the tree.

She sent them to Christian, thinking about the reindeer as she did so. Her plans to visit the farm where the reindeer lived. With Duran. Try as she might, she couldn't fight the little twist of excitement in her belly. Her attraction to Duran might be a problem eventually, but for now, she was enjoying that silly crush feeling. She hadn't felt even a tickle of this sort of attraction in a long time, and as long as she remembered nothing could come of hanging out with Duran while she was here, it wasn't a problem.

A roaring fire blazed across the room from the wall of windows at the back of the lodge. McKenzie wound her way through the artfully arranged furniture and dropped her backpack in a comfortable-looking padded chair by the fireplace. She took another look at the tree and let herself just enjoy the thrill of the moment, of the festive atmosphere, before going to find the coffee.

"Good morning!"

McKenzie glanced at the woman behind the reception counter as she approached what appeared to be a very high-tech coffee machine. Who knew? Maybe it made lattes and espressos and plucked stars from the sky, too.

"Good morning," she said to the woman.

"It's scarier than it looks." The woman slipped out from behind the counter. "Just choose a cup. Choose which drink you'd like and press it. Hit start."

"Nice." McKenzie nodded.

"We get our coffee from Caffeinated Bliss. It's very good."

"I was there yesterday."

"Good." The woman, skinny black jeans tucked into long black boots with a long red tunic on top, folded her arms over her chest. "Here on vacation?"

"No. Actually." McKenzie studied the coffee contraption, selected a large to-go cup, and pressed the mocha button before hitting start. She whirled around now to look at the woman. "I'm here to meet with the manager."

"Our manager?"

"Yes."

"Oh. Okay. Well, he's in his office. Been on the phone since he came in. Do you have a set time?"

"It was yesterday." McKenzie shrugged as if to say no big deal. "He called to reschedule after a family emergency."

"Mmm." The woman nodded. "Big emergency. Connie Vahle is the kindergarten teacher. Whoever steps in to sub for her has big shoes to fill."

"I'm sorry she fell," McKenzie said sincerely.

"I'm Anita," the woman told her. "Are you heading out now?"

"No." McKenzie pointed in the general direction of the fireplace. "I'm going to check email and see about working for a bit over by the fireplace."

"Okay. Let me check and see how he's coming. Remind him to get in touch with you."

"It's fine," McKenzie assured her. "I'm not in a hurry."

"Good." Anita nodded. "That's the best way to visit Amesbury. No hurries. No worries."

"I'm McKenzie." She offered her hand, pleased when Anita grasped it easily and shook.

"There's a lot to see out there." Anita nodded her head to the main door. "If you get caught up on email."

"I was out for a while yesterday. With my very own tour guide."

"Oh? Who's that?"

"Duran?"

The machine let out a steamy hiss. McKenzie noticed the light had turned off, and her paper cup now steamed. She picked it up and then reached for a lid.

"Duran Carey?" Anita grinned. "How lucky for you to get a personal tour of Amesbury from such a sweetheart."

McKenzie couldn't argue with that. Duran had been nice, fun. And definitely sweet to walk her back to the lodge.

"My youngest son went to school with Duran," Anita told her. "Hightailed it outta Amesbury for college and never came back."

"Duran said most of his friends left after college."

Anita smiled sadly. "My sons are in Minnesota. But Duran's pretty good at making the rounds to visit with all of us orphaned, abandoned parents."

McKenzie laughed quietly.

"I'll let you get to work." Anita headed back behind the counter. "It's nice to meet you."

"You, too." McKenzie found a sleeve for her cup, slipped it on, and then carried it over to her seat by the fireplace. Once she was settled with her coffee on the table at her side and her laptop booted up and ready for work, she glanced at her phone.

She wasn't in a hurry to get her meeting done. Technically, she had several days if the manager needed that much time to take care of things on his end. However, she didn't like having to wait to contact Duran about the rest of her day.

Realizing she was considering texting him just to say good morning, she forced herself to put the phone down and get to work.

CHAPTER TEN

DURAN

Their argument had escalated. As far as Duran could tell, his mom had launched an attack on his dad after dinner for making a mess on the stovetop. And his dad had countered with complaints that his favorite sweater was still at the dry cleaners.

There was more to it, but Duran wasn't interested in hearing it. His parents had been married for thirty-five years, and they were passionate. About everything. Each other. Duran. The Amesbury community. Fighting.

They would get over it. Duran knew that. But he had no intention of getting involved or choosing sides. Instead of listening to his dad grumble throughout the morning, he busied himself with cleaning. First the restroom; something he hated doing but also something that needed to be done. Then he mopped the floor a bit at a time, careful of any customers browsing.

When he had finished that job, he dismantled a window display and put the merchandise back. That ski display had been up for three weeks; he was tired of looking at it, and he was running out of things to keep him away from his dad's foul mood. Once the skis and the parkas and accessories had been returned to their rightful places, he gathered what he would need to make a Christmas window display, complete with a skinny tree, a family of headless mannequins—he hated them—and a couple of sleds. He found empty boxes his mom had wrapped a few years ago in bright reds and golds and added those to his pile.

Staying busy would be the only way to keep his mind off McKenzie. He had enjoyed the time spent with her the night before. So much so that he had given up worrying about how cliché it seemed; why not just have fun and savor the moment? It wasn't like he was going to fall in love with her and pine for her when she went back home. They could be adults and experience some holiday activities together without catching feelings.

Slopes was busy with the holiday season in full swing. Eventually, his dad's sour mood faded, and he was his usual jovial self with their customers and even Duran. He'd chosen a pop holiday playlist for the day, and often times, Duran heard him humming along when he wasn't helping customers.

Duran tried to make sure he grabbed the phone anytime it rang, just in case it was his mom. No need for them to rehash their argument during business hours. It crossed his mind, too, that he might answer the phone and hear McKenzie's voice on the other end. He knew that was dumb; after all, he'd given her his cell number and she hadn't called.

Still, it was kind of fun to go about his day wondering about her, wondering what she was doing. He was glad to have the afternoon off; his dad always hired part time help for the holidays. Duran had plans for McKenzie; he would make sure she experienced a full Amesbury Christmas before she headed home. However, he didn't want to share that information with his parents. They would probably make more of it than there was, and with the way his mind was running so far ahead of him with thoughts of McKenzie, he didn't need any help with that.

"What's with the smile on your face today?"

He looked at his dad, startled by his out of the blue question. The woman his dad had just waited on walked out the door with her big green Slopes shopping bag in hand. The bell above the door twinkled. Leona Lewis sang about one more sleep until Christmas.

"What?" He didn't need his dad to repeat the question. He'd heard him loud and clear. Duran just wanted a second to figure out how to answer him.

"You look happy." His dad narrowed his eyes at him as if being happy was suspicious behavior.

"It's...Christmas time?" Duran shrugged.

His dad shook his head. "Nope. More to it than that."

"Maybe *you're* feeling better today and projecting on me," he suggested.

"Rumor has it you shared a table with a pretty little blonde at Caffeinated Bliss yesterday at lunch."

Duran rolled his eyes. Small town living at its best.

"What's her name?"

"She's here on business," he told his dad, cringing inside at his words. Why start with that? He almost sounded defensive, even to his own ears. As if he was warning his dad not to push a matchmaker move because McKenzie wouldn't be around long. Why hadn't he just told him the truth? Sure, McKenzie was a pretty blonde, but she'd also been reading the book Duran had been waiting for all year.

"Where's she from?"

"Don't know." Duran leaned on the counter. "She's here to scout the area for a conference for her business."

"Mmm." His dad nodded. "If that went well, she could potentially be back in the area sometime."

Duran had to laugh. This was proof that as frustrated as his dad got with his mom—and vice versa—the man believed in love. Well, that and his parents always liked to drop hints that they hoped they would have grandchildren someday.

"Her name's McKenzie, and she's reading the new Ford Bishop book." He tossed his hands up as if to say no big deal. "We talked about it over my lunch."

"So you have a common interest."

"You're worse than Mom," he mumbled.

"Wanna know what I think?"

"Not really, no." Duran grinned. "But you're gonna tell me."

"I am." His dad nodded. "Amesbury's a small place."

"No kidding," Duran mumbled. He was surprised his dad hadn't mentioned the after dark tour of Amesbury Duran had given McKenzie. He wouldn't flinch if he did; surely someone had seen them and told his parents. Maybe his dad was saving that for his trump card.

"You know everyone here, Duran." His dad glanced at the door when the bells twinkled. "There're some great girls here, but you know them all so well, you can't date them."

Okay, his dad had a point there, even if Duran didn't like where he was going with his comments.

"You want to settle down someday, don't you?"

"You say that like I'm thirty-five."

"Your mom and I won't be around forever, Duran. We want you to be happy."

Wow. Now his dad was getting philosophical on him.

"Odds are you're not gonna fall in love with the girl next door."

"Well, I hope not, because as nice as Therese is, she also just celebrated her sixtieth birthday."

His dad gave him a stern look.

"You know what I'm saying."

Duran sighed and looked away. He did know what his dad was saying, but that didn't mean he wanted to think about this stuff. Not now. He had plenty of time to find Mrs. Right. He had time to fall in love. To get married and start a family.

Just because he met a pretty blonde, just because they had clicked and enjoyed each other's company, didn't have to mean anything.

"Excuse me, where can I find the boots in the window display?"

Duran almost groaned in relief as his dad turned his attention to the customer on the other side of the counter. His dad—his parents—meant well. But he wasn't ready for that conversation.

And even if he was, even if he did have a little crush on McKenzie, he had no desire to share that or her with anyone just yet.

His phone buzzed in his pocket. He turned away from the counter and wandered through the men's clothing as he slipped it out to look at it.

If I have to talk to Santa, you do, too.

CHAPTER ELEVEN

But Santa knows me.

McKenzie laughed softly.

Hmm. Does that mean you're on the naughty list?

She tapped out her answer and set her phone down just as it rang. Holding her breath, she snatched it up, hoping it was Duran. The number was somewhat familiar, but Duran's name wasn't on the screen. Slightly disappointed, McKenzie cleared her throat and tapped the screen to answer the call.

"Hello?"

"McKenzie Noble? This is Jarrett Hunt."

Naturally, she had finally stopped arguing with herself and texted Duran to start a conversation with him. And now Jarrett Hunt was calling. Oh well; she was in Amesbury to meet with Jarrett Hunt. Once this part of her trip was settled, she would have time to herself to do whatever she wanted.

"Hi, Jarrett."

"I am so sorry for the delay in getting back to you." The guy sounded sincere, as well as completely strung out.

"It's no trouble."

Her phone buzzed with what she hoped was an incoming text from Duran. She fisted her fingers and reminded herself she could text him later. Right now, she was working, just as he was.

"I'm sure you're busy at the moment, but—"

"Actually, I'm sitting in the lobby of the lodge working. I can be free anytime."

"Really?" He laughed. "Mmm. Let me guess. By the fireplace where you have a beautiful view of the tree and the wall of windows in the back."

"You are correct."

"Stay put, and I'll be out in a few minutes."

"Perfect. Thank you."

She ended the call and peeked at Duran's text even after telling herself she would wait until she had her laptop packed up.

Haven't been on the naughty list since I was fourteen.

Her fingertips tingled. She wanted to text back immediately. What had Duran Carey done to get on the naughty list at fourteen? Still, as curious as she was, she put her phone down and packed up her backpack.

Well, now, I'm very curious about what you did at fourteen. Heading into my meeting now.

The phone buzzed in her hand, but it was simply Duran liking her message. If she were being honest with herself, she would have to admit she'd thought about him as she worked. She'd thought about him a lot. Maybe as much as she'd thought about work.

The evening before, wandering around Amesbury with him, had been a little bit magical. She was still trying to figure out if it was the guy or the setting that had warmed her heart. As long as she'd considered the possibilities, all she had come up with was that she had enjoyed both equally.

She was looking forward to hanging out with him after her meeting. Maybe she would even surprise him and walk down to his family's store. She could do a little shopping while she was there.

"McKenzie?"

"Hi, yes." She flashed a smile at the man who approached her with a sheepish smile of his own. Dropping her phone in a side pocket of her bag, she climbed gracefully to her feet and shook the guy's hand. "McKenzie Noble."

"Jarrett Hunt." He pumped her hand with a strong shake. "If you want to bring your bag to my office, you can leave it there and we can look at the conference rooms."

"Thank you." She nodded, grabbed the bag and her empty coffee cup, and followed the guy back across the lobby and past the reception desk. She guessed him to be mid-forties.

Dressed in denim, sensible hiking boots, and a green sweater, he looked festive without being over-the-top. She liked that; the lodge was rustic and homey, rather than uptight and stuffy. From what she'd seen so far, Amesbury seemed like a good fit for the IEC conference.

Not that IEC wouldn't choose a big city venue. Maybe McKenzie was projecting her likes on the company. She reminded herself to be careful in relaying information to Lena as she followed Jarrett Hunt into an office just down the hall.

"You're welcome to leave your things here," he told her. "They'll be fine."

"Thank you." She nodded and put her backpack down. "How's your mother-in-law?"

Jarrett sighed and pinched the bridge of his nose, but he still managed a small smile. McKenzie pulled her phone from her bag and stuck it in her back pocket.

"Stubborn," he answered. "Insisting she's fine. Even though she's in the hospital."

"I'm so sorry to hear that."

"They'll be moving her to rehab at Sedgwick Mountain Care. She's not happy about that."

McKenzie had a grandmother in a nursing home, so she understood the hardship for Jarrett's mother-in-law and the rest of his family.

"At least it'll just be for rehab."

"Very true," he agreed. "She's a kindergarten teacher. And she loves her kids. She's worried to death about how they'll handle all the Christmas activities without her there."

"Well, I hope someone can help her out."

Jarrett nodded. "I'm sure they'll get it figured out. That's one of the nice things about Amesbury. Now. Let's talk about you and IEC."

"Inovial is in the business of textbooks and technology for students. We do annual conferences for educational professionals, and we're interested in hosting here in Amesbury."

"That's fantastic." Jarrett gestured for her to follow him back into the hallway. "What kind of numbers does your conference generally draw?"

"The average for the last three years is around a hundred."

"We have a hundred and fifty rooms, and we have seven ballrooms that serve as conference rooms."

McKenzie nodded; she and Lena had done the minimum amount of research on Sterling Lodge in Amesbury before narrowing their decision down to this one and one other mountain lodge in Utah. She and a coworker had drawn straws to see who went to Montana and who went to Utah. At the time, she had no preference, assuming both sites would be beautiful. Now that she was here in Amesbury, now that she'd met Duran Carey, she was glad she'd drawn Amesbury.

"We have a steakhouse here in the lodge," Jarrett continued. "Or you can cater lunches in from any of the businesses here in town. We work with all of them."

"Nice," she said with a nod. She liked the close-knit feel of community.

"Coffees and breakfast juices are included in the rental fee. Sound system, technology, wi-fi..."

He continued his pitch as he escorted her around the lodge, showing her all seven ballrooms and the steakhouse. She made notes on her phone, things she wanted to make sure and share with Lena. If it were her choice, she would easily decide Sterling Lodge in Amesbury was the perfect place to host a conference. But she was well aware that the lodge in Utah might be just as perfect. All she could do was share her findings with Lena and hope for the best.

Aware that hoping for the best meant hoping for Amesbury just so she would have another opportunity sometime in the foreseeable future to see Duran, she followed Jarrett outside, shivering as he pointed out the mountain view from the patio. She liked the fire pit and Adirondack chairs around it, but thought it was too cold at this time of year to enjoy that particular amenity.

Back in Jarrett's office, McKenzie shook his hand again and told him she would be reporting back to her supervisor. Jarrett apologized again for having to change their meeting time, but McKenzie waved his words off, sharing positive thoughts for his mother-in-law's recovery.

She left the meeting feeling confident it had gone well, confident that she could sell Sterling Lodge in Amesbury to Lena, and headed back to her room. Grabbing her coat, she set her backpack in the closet, slipped into the bathroom to take care of business which, of course, included freshening up her lip gloss, and then headed out on a mission to find Duran.

CHAPTER TWELVE

Duran

"Be with you in just a second!" Duran called when the bells over the door jingled. His dad had slipped out to grab a bite to eat, so until Ellen—the part-timer—came in, Duran was flying solo. His current customer was trying on a pair of snow boots, but Duran thought the guy was close to making his decision and buying them.

Gene Autry's "Rudolph the Red-Nosed Reindeer" played around them as the guy tugged the boots off and tucked them back in the box.

"I'll take 'em."

Duran nodded as the guy shoved the box at him.

"Can I get you anything else?" he asked. "What about socks?"

He had no idea what the guy planned to do in the snow boots, but Duran did know that it could get dangerously cold out there this time of year.

"I'm gonna look around a bit, if that's okay."

"Take your time," Duran told him. "I'll put the boots up on the counter."

He wondered what time it was as he carried the box to the counter and set it down. How had McKenzie's meeting gone? Did her company have other sites in mind to host their conference? He hoped not, but it seemed probable. It would come down to fees and amenities, as any business decision should.

But Duran wished Sterling Lodge was the only conference center in the running.

He hadn't seen the last customer come in, so he wandered the store now, looking for him or her. He caught sight of the blond hair and coat in the women's clothing and moseyed up to stand beside McKenzie. It wasn't that he doubted she would be here today, that she would want to see him. Not after hanging out last night.

But still, seeing her here in the store made him breathe easier than he had all day. That was saying something, considering the odds were his dad would return while she was here. He would insist on introducing himself, embarrassing Duran, as if he couldn't find his own dates.

Not that he and McKenzie were dating.

Hard to do that when she wasn't a local.

"Hey."

"Hi!"

Duran had assumed last night that the twinkle in her eyes related directly to the holiday atmosphere. After all, he had seen Santa's little village year after year after year, and he still found it a little magical. But standing here in his family store, McKenzie's eyes had that same twinkle, her face a mask of wonder. She looked ready for anything, any sort of adventure he might pose.

"How'd the meeting go?"

"Really well," she answered. "I just spoke with my supervisor before I came in."

"Good." He nodded. "What're we up against? Boston? Denver?"

"Utah."

"Oh." Duran winced. "That's hard. Ever been there?"

"No."

"There are some beautiful places there, too."

"Well, let's hope I sold Amesbury."

He laughed softly.

"I like the store," she announced with a sweeping look around.

"Yeah? How about the Christmas window display?"

"Did you do it?"

"This morning."

"I like it," she answered. "Which reminds me. Naughty list at fourteen."

Duran groaned and hunched his shoulders wishing he could hide.

"I might have stolen a snowmobile. For a joyride."

"You *might* have stolen a snowmobile."

"Me and some buddies," he admitted. "From my friend's dad."

"Did he press charges?"

"No. But we did wreck it. So. Naughty list."

"Oh, shoot!"

"How about you?"

"Never driven a snowmobile."

"Naughty list?"

"Mmm." She frowned. "Seven? Got in trouble for playing with my aunt's makeup."

"Like you did your face?"

"My face and a few walls."

"Ooh." He shook his head. "As soon as my dad gets back from his lunch, I can get out of here."

"No hurry."

"Mm-hmm. We're going to see Santa, remember?"

"Sure. Long as you talk to him, too."

"Did you read more last night?"

"Maybe."

"I'm on chapter seventeen," he told her.

"Wow. I'm on thirteen."

"Do you want to have dinner tonight?"

He wasn't sure where the question had come from, but he was glad he had blurted it out.

"Yes. I'd like that."

"My place?" he suggested, hoping he wasn't being too forward. "I'm a block west of Main."

"Yeah." She nodded. "Sounds good."

"Maybe you shouldn't comment until after I cook for you."

"I'm going to trust you," she said simply. "Either you can cook, or you've got guts inviting me over when you can't."

"I could scramble to pick up takeout and pretend I fixed it."

"You could," she agreed. "But I don't think you will."

The bells twinkled again. Duran glanced at the door to see his dad come inside, phone pressed to his ear.

"Oh, no." He sighed.

"What's wrong?"

"He's on the phone," he said quietly.

"And that's a bad thing?"

"He and my mom have been at a standoff for several hours now. He's grouchy when they fight."

McKenzie's laughter loosened the knots in his stomach.

"Do they fight a lot?"

"No," he admitted. "But when they do, I regret being an only child as well as working with my dad."

His dad ended his phone call and put his cell on the counter as he unzipped his coat.

"Was that Mom?" Duran asked.

His dad's eye roll was answer enough.

"Dorothy Adair was going to take over, but she's come down with pneumonia since yesterday."

"Great." Duran mumbled. He felt McKenzie's eyes on him. He reached for her hand, as he had last night. But this time, neither of them had gloves on. The skin-to-skin contact jolted him. Her hand was warm, her skin soft.

"Is this your friend?"

Duran bit down on his response. He didn't want to be rude, but he hoped his dad didn't say something to embarrass him.

"Dad, this is McKenzie..."

"Noble," she supplied her last name. "McKenzie Noble."

"McKenzie, this is my dad, Gabe Carey."

"Nice to meet you, Mr. Carey."

"Please call me Gabe," his dad answered as he reached to shake McKenzie's hand. Duran hoped he hadn't noticed they were holding hands a second ago. It meant nothing, after all.

"Gabe." She nodded.

"Did you enjoy your tour of Amesbury last night?"

Duran narrowed his eyes at his dad, wondering who had seen them and why his dad had waited until now to ambush him with that knowledge.

"I did," McKenzie answered, apparently unfazed by his question. "It's a beautiful town."

"It is, I agree," his dad said simply. "It's beautiful in the off-season, too."

"I'm from Southern Illinois," she told them both. "We have cute little town squares. But no mountains in the background."

"Get outta here," his dad told him with a wink. Duran hoped McKenzie hadn't seen it.

"Call me if you get too busy."

His dad waved him away, reminding him Ellen would be in within minutes.

"Let's go see Santa," Duran suggested to McKenzie.

"Do I get to ask him about your grand theft auto days?"

"Absolutely not."

He grabbed his coat from under the counter and pulled it on.

"If you talk to your mother, tell her I'm packed, and I'm leaving tomorrow."

Duran narrowed his eyes at his dad as he and McKenzie approached the door.

"I will not be talking to Mom," he promised his dad. "Do you want to grab some coffee first?"

"No, thanks."

"Hot chocolate? We have a little hot chocolate bar in the back of the store."

"I'm good for now, thanks."

"Then let's go see the man with the bag."

CHAPTER THIRTEEN

MᴄKᴇɴᴢɪᴇ

Santa did indeed know Duran, but McKenzie didn't bring up the snowmobile incident. Santa's beard, belly, and rosy cheeks certainly seemed to be the real thing, making McKenzie again think about Hallmark Christmas movies and magical Santas sharing their wisdom. McKenzie had nothing on her heart that she needed to discuss with him, so she wouldn't be able to test that particular festive detail.

Rather than doing a picture in his lap, she and Duran stood with Santa between them for a photo. While they waited for their picture to print, the two of them watched several little kids scampering around, excited for their turn to talk to Santa. McKenzie did send Christian a Snapchat of Santa's village and a video capturing the buzz of excitement in the air.

After visiting Santa, Duran led her around the small town away from Main Street. McKenzie was thrilled to see that the rest of the town was just as charming as Main. There were more small bakeries and diners. Boutiques for women, children, even pets. True to his word, Duran walked her by Don Kirkpatrick's house and pointed out Marvin, the German Shepherd, who watched them vigilantly through the window. And Marvin did, indeed, have his own jail cell at the police station, complete with a big comfy-looking dog bed and bowls for food and water. When McKenzie laughed, honestly surprised that Duran hadn't been fibbing, he admitted that the chief of police was Don Kirkpatrick's brother.

They wandered north into the foothill area of the mountains, but she wasn't prepared for any hard-core hiking. Rather, she simply stared up at the snow-covered peaks in wonder.

She took several pictures of the mountains, of Amesbury from where they stood, and even a few of Duran. At the very least, they could stay in touch as friends.

"How about hot chocolate now?" he suggested.

"I could do that now," she agreed. Even with her coat zipped up and her thick wool socks inside her boots, she was cold. They walked another block east and then circled back around to Main; McKenzie eating up the cute little houses decorated for Christmas.

"Do you talk to your mom?" she asked after they'd walked in silence for a while.

"Hmm?" Duran stirred from his thoughts.

"The way your dad made it sound..." She trailed off, uncertain if she should continue. Duran's dad had said he was packed and leaving. That sounded ominous to her. But Duran didn't seem all that concerned about it.

"Oh." His smile puffed his cheeks up a bit. He shook his head. "So, the deal is, they have a trip planned. A cruise for their thirty-fifth wedding anniversary for the holidays. And my mom's making noise about being needed at work, thinking she should stay here."

"Uh-oh."

"Yeah. It's happened before. But this vacation is bigger. And more expensive. So Dad's not happy with her."

"Where does she work?"

"She's the secretary at St. Anne's. Where Mrs. Vahle is the kindergarten teacher."

"Oh boy." McKenzie nodded as the situation clicked into place for her. "She wants to stick around and help out with the Christmas program and stuff for the kids."

"For the kids," he agreed, "and also, the kids take their show on the road and present it at the nursing home."

"Oh."

"So, the kids get excited about performing. And the residents at the nursing home enjoy seeing the kids."

"And there's no one else to step up and help out?"

"Apparently not."

"Still, your mom deserves to go on her vacation with your dad."

"Yeah. And I'm afraid this time he will go without her."

"Yikes."

She looked up to see they were back on Main Street, at the end of the main thoroughfare where his family's store was situated. Assuming he was taking her to Caffeinated Bliss, McKenzie was happy to keep walking.

"What if..." She hesitated and sank her teeth into her lower lip. Nope. Not her place. She should just walk away from this and let the situation play out however it played out.

"What if?"

She looked up at him to find him watching her with interest.

"What all does it entail?"

"The program?" He frowned. "The kids do a little live nativity scene. And then they sing a few songs."

"That's it?"

"I think so." He nodded. "Why?"

"There's no...like...substitute teaching or anything?"

"No. The kids will be on Christmas break next week. So, not until after the break."

"What if you did it?"

"What?"

"Show up and watch the kids. Surely, they've rehearsed it a hundred times."

"But they're kindergarteners. Imagine the chaos."

She shrugged at him with a smile. "My guess is it's always chaos. And that's probably half the fun for the residents at the nursing home."

Duran studied her face so intently, McKenzie felt herself blush.

"I mean, you could do it. You know. If you weren't busy. It would take a load off your mom, and then your parents could take their trip and have a good time." She shrugged. "But I get it. It's the holiday season. You probably have a million things to do."

"Actually." He shook his head as they neared the coffee shop and bookstore where they'd first met just yesterday. McKenzie had to marvel at that thought for a second. She felt like she had known Duran for years instead of a matter of hours. "I really don't have that much going on."

She peeked at him as they approached the counter.

"How's the book?" the guy at the counter asked them. "I know you were both reading it yesterday when you were here."

"Good." Duran nodded. "The problem is it's so good, I read it too fast."

"And then I have to wait another year for the next one," McKenzie added on.

"Exactly."

The guy winced and nodded. "The problem with reading a series before it's completed. What can I get you?"

They ordered hot chocolates and stood at the counter discussing other authors they enjoyed until the guy slid their cups to them over the counter. Duran tapped his credit card on the machine, waved away the receipt, and then dropped a couple of bucks in a jar on the counter for a tip.

"You know what? You're right," Duran announced when they were seated at the same table where they had talked yesterday. "I could offer to help. The show must go on. And Mom and Dad can enjoy their cruise."

McKenzie smiled, happy that Duran thought her idea would work. Surely it would make him feel good to smooth out the situation with his parents.

"Thanks for suggesting that." He met her eyes over his cup as he took a sip of his drink.

"Will it be an issue? Having someone outside the school system work with the kids?"

"Shouldn't be," he answered. "Dad and I've been around a lot to help with different events. Not sure why it never occurred to me before now to volunteer."

"Good."

"When do you fly home?"

"Sunday evening."

His smile brightened enough that she narrowed her eyes at him suspiciously.

"What?"

"You could come and see the program." He quirked an eyebrow at her.

"I'd love to," she answered with genuine enthusiasm. "I would really love that, Duran."

"Perfect." He nodded. "I'll call Mom and make sure it'll work for me to volunteer. And I'll get the correct time of the program."

She sipped her hot chocolate and then stirred it with a peppermint stick.

"Guess this is where the similarities between real life and a Hallmark movie stop."

His laugh drew her gaze away from her drink. "How so?"

"Well, if this were a movie, I'd be the one to sweep in and save the community Christmas program."

"Well, you were hero-adjacent."

She snorted and rolled her eyes. "Two degrees of separation?"

"Something like that," he said with a nod. "So, you'll come to dinner tonight?"

"I will."

"Can I pick you up?"

"I can walk." She shook her head. "In fact, I need to with all the sweet treats I've had since I got here."

"Okay." He nodded. "But either I drive you back to the lodge or I walk with you."

She considered arguing, but she didn't.

And it wasn't the resolute look on his face that stopped her, either.

It was the idea that she would have more time with him if he took her back to the lodge.

CHAPTER FOURTEEN

McKenzie had gone back to the lodge after they talked over hot chocolate. She mentioned a bit of work she should do on her laptop, and she wanted to touch base with her supervisor again. Duran headed back to Slopes to check on his dad and Ellen and make sure they weren't too busy. While there was a steady stream of customers in and out even while Duran was there checking in, Dad and Ellen seemed to have everything under control.

Before he left, he did take two phone calls for his dad— neither of which was his mom—and ring one customer up. Duran liked Christmas, so he was always happy to help someone with a purchase and wish him or her a Merry Christmas as he or she left. But today, there was something extra cheerful about his greeting. He knew it came from that warm place inside his heart. And the warm place inside his heart was all about a businesswoman in town from Southern Illinois.

Next week, when his parents were on their cruise, when McKenzie was gone, and it was Christmas, that festive holiday magic might just sour into a big fat bah humbug. But for now, he was going to enjoy every moment he had with her.

When he left Slopes, he took his SUV and drove to the school. Best to talk to his mom now and hopefully get the situation settled so she could go home and finish packing. And there would be peace at the Carey home. That thought made him laugh as he parked in the street across from the big, white-bricked building.

It was just after three, so school had let out already. But as usual when he happened to drop by here, there were still kids here and there. Some of them were probably in detention. Duran laughed to himself as he entered through the main doors. He'd had detention a time or two, but he hadn't shared that with McKenzie. Technically, he supposed the snowmobile theft was probably his biggest offense. McKenzie wouldn't be interested in the times he got in trouble for not returning homework on time or for talking in class.

"Hi."

He looked up at the little boy standing in the doorway of the gymnasium. The kid leaned in the doorframe, with his feet crossed and a basketball tucked to his side, under his arm. Short enough he was probably only five or six-years-old. But the athletic pose suggested he had an older sibling who played basketball.

"Hi."

"Are you here to play?"

"No." Duran laughed. If he didn't have dinner plans with McKenzie, he might have said yes and stayed to shoot a few baskets with the kid.

"Do you go to school here?"

He barked another laugh. "I used to."

"I'm in kindergarten," the kid announced. Duran looked him over, thinking if things worked out, he would be directing the kid in the program in another day.

"I'm looking for Mrs. Carey."

"She's in the office," the kid said with a shrug. "Are you Mr. Carey?"

"No." Duran tucked his hands in his pockets. "Mrs. Carey is my mom."

"She has a kid?"

"She does."

"Wow." The little boy shook his head as if to convey his shock.

"See ya later, okay?"

"Yeah. I'm gonna shoot hoops." The kid nodded his head at the gym behind him. Duran assumed he was in afters chool care and probably shouldn't be in the doorway talking to just anyone who walked inside.

"Have fun."

The echo of the kid dribbling the ball once and then twice followed Duran down the hall. When the dribbling stopped, Duran could only imagine the ball got away from the kid. He wondered who his older siblings were, if he knew any of them. The sound of Christmas music carried down the hall as he made his way to the office.

Two tween girls were hanging with his mom when he knocked on her door and stepped inside the small room.

"Hi." His mom gave him a suspicious smile. He felt the girls checking him out, not sure whether he should be amused or concerned.

"Bye, Mrs. Carey!" they chimed in unison as they hurried out the door.

"What're you doing here?"

Before he could answer his mom, she dropped her head back and groaned out loud.

"Your dad sent you here, didn't he? To plead his case about the cruise."

Duran held his hands up, palms out, to stop her.

"I have an idea," he said simply. "Actually, it wasn't my idea, but I think it'll work."

"What?" She tipped her head and stared at him with that pre-angry look she usually aimed at his dad. Duran thought his parents made an attractive couple, but he also thought they both looked stressed, and both could use a little time away.

"Let me do it."

"Do what?" She shook her head.

"Handle the program."

"Duran."

"Seriously, Mom. What is it? One more rehearsal tomorrow? The program for the parents and families Friday night. And the nursing home on Saturday afternoon?"

"Yeah. But—"

"I think it would work. I mean, it's not like much changes year to year, right? I've seen the program a hundred times."

"Everything changes year to year, Duran. Because each new class is different, and kids are different, and you can't anticipate what's going to happen."

"I think I can handle it."

His mom sighed. "Tell him I'll go," she mumbled.

"What?"

"If this wasn't your idea, I'm assuming your dad put you up to it. So tell him I'll go. I'm tired of fighting with him about it. They'll just have to cancel everything."

"It wasn't Dad's idea," Duran corrected her. "And I absolutely want to do this."

"Whose idea was it then?"

"Why does that matter?"

"I just don't like your dad manipulating you or me—"

"It wasn't dad's idea. I promise."

His mom pushed her chair back and stood, intense eyes drilling into him. And then suddenly, the intense frown was gone, and she wore a slight, pleased smile.

"What?" he asked, suddenly suspicious of her now.

"Does this have anything to do with a pretty little blond tourist?"

"She's not a tourist," he answered. He didn't have time to do the innocent dance and pretend like he didn't know who she was talking about. If he planned to fix dinner for McKenzie tonight, he needed to get to the market and get home.

"No?"

"She's in town on business, and she might have put a bug in my ear."

"You don't have to do this, Duran."

"I want to, Mom."

"Is she planning to help you?"

"No. But she is planning to come and see the program."

"You might need help. Keeping an eye on seventeen five-year-olds can be like herding cats."

"I'll enlist a parent if I need help."

Apparently ready to give in, his mom's smile turned appreciative as she wrapped him in a hug.

"Thank you, Duran."

"You're welcome." He hugged her back. "Go home and finish packing."

"Wanna come over tonight? Get a pizza?"

He felt a pang of guilt. It was the usual when either he or his parents were leaving town, whether for a weekend or a longer trip. They always hung out and shared a pizza for dinner.

"Um." He raised his eyebrows. "I...have plans."

She grinned up at him, almost making him regret telling her the truth.

"And do they involve a pretty little blond businesswoman?"

"Call me in the morning." He leaned over to drop a kiss on his mom's cheek. "Bye, Mom."

CHAPTER FIFTEEN

McKenzie

She wasn't surprised to see white Christmas lights around the front door of Duran's townhouse. Through the front window, she saw the tree, also covered in twinkling white lights. Nope, not surprised at all. The guy had made it clear that he liked the Christmas season; he had Christmas spirit.

McKenzie stood on the sidewalk in front of the modern, trendy townhouse and admired the lights for a moment. Pleased. As if it made any difference in the world, as if she wouldn't be packing her bags and heading home in a few days, she was ridiculously pleased with her first look at Duran Carey's house.

Deciding she had better knock before one of his neighbors saw her outside and assumed she was casing the neighborhood, she laughed to herself as she hurried up the walk to the door. Sure, Duran was good-looking. Yes, in the short amount of time she'd known him she had grown to like him. And no, she wasn't looking forward to returning home and leaving him, his world, behind. But on the other hand, it warmed her heart to know there were guys like him out there.

Maybe she would find someone like him back home.

That thought didn't sit well with her, so she gave herself a mental shake as she knocked on his door. She heard Kelly Clarkson signing Christmas music, noticed when it was turned down a bit, and then there he was, opening the door and inviting her inside.

"Hi." Feeling shy suddenly, McKenzie ducked her head as she entered. Duran leaned around her to close the door.

"Hi. I'm glad you're here."

"Thanks."

"Let me take your coat," he offered. McKenzie slipped it off her shoulders and looked around the living area as he took it from her. "How was the walk?"

"Nice, actually." She watched him hang her coat on a stand near the door. "It's so peaceful with the lights and the Christmas music."

"It is," he agreed. "I hope you like Italian food."

"Doesn't everyone?"

"Dinner's almost ready. Make yourself at home. I'll be right back."

McKenzie nodded and turned to his tree as he disappeared into what she assumed was the kitchen. Tall and skinny, the tree towered a bit over her head. Decorated in white lights and ornaments of all shapes and colors, it made her think of home. Christian had liked the Snapchats she had sent him of all the holiday clichés around town. And he had sent her a few pictures of Christmas trees and decorations from home.

She missed her family, especially since it was the holiday season. But the more she thought about leaving Amesbury, leaving Duran, the worse she felt.

"Eggnog?"

She turned to him with a laugh as Duran approached, a cute Christmas mug in hand.

"It's actually cheater eggnog," he promised. "Melted ice cream. No actual raw eggs."

"Interesting." She took the mug from him and studied the creamy-looking contents. "I've actually never had eggnog."

"No?"

"Nope."

He watched her take a sip, visibly relieved when she swallowed and smiled at him.

"I talked to my mom," he told her. "Told her I'd take over the program so she could stop worrying."

"And how did that go?"

"Well, at first, she assumed Dad put me up to it. That I didn't really want to do it."

"Uh-oh."

Duran laughed and shook his head. "No, I convinced her it wasn't dad. But somehow, she figured out it was connected to the pretty little blond tourist everyone's seen in town."

McKenzie laughed as she tried to swallow. Coughing a bit, she cleared her throat and met his eyes.

"Small town," he reminded her.

"Yeah." She licked her lips, feeling a little shy again. "I sent our selfie with Barry and Elvis to a friend."

"And?" He quirked an eyebrow at her.

She nodded. "Um...let's see...She commented on the reindeer. The Christmas lights in the background. The snow. And you."

"Me," he repeated.

"You." She nodded.

"Like, she said *the reindeer are easier on the eyes than that guy*?"

McKenzie chuckled. "No. More like I must be in a Christmas movie, complete with a Hollywood hottie."

"Hollywood hottie." He grinned. "I kind of like that."

Eyes locked with his, heat zinged through her fingers and toes. Her belly flip-flopped a bit. This silly little crush could easily get out of hand. Did he have mistletoe anywhere? Because Duran seemed to be the sort of guy who would kiss her under the mistletoe.

Her cheeks flushed with heat at the thought of kissing him. What if she broke the eye contact and looked at his lips? What if he knew she was thinking about kissing him?

A loud beep interrupted the moment.

"Dinner," he announced, but he spoke softly, as if he, too, had been caught up in thoughts of kissing. He cleared his throat. "Is the music okay? Too loud?"

"It's perfect," she answered as she followed him to the kitchen. The smell of garlic hung in the air, but it was especially strong in the kitchen. McKenzie touched her belly when it growled.

"My mom's recipe," he told her. "But I did fix it."

Her eyes grew wide as he pulled a baking dish of lasagna from the oven.

"Oh, wow. That looks so good."

"Well." He nodded his head back and forth with a smile. "Mom's is always good. So, fingers crossed."

McKenzie offered to help, but he waved her off. The table was already set. No romantic candlelight, no wine glasses. And yet, this felt more comfortable, more right, than any date she had been on in recent history.

Seated together at the table, Duran dug into the lasagna and pronounced it almost as good as his mom's.

"Well, then hers must be heavenly," she told him as she took her first bite.

"So, tomorrow I'll have to be at the school for one last rehearsal."

"Are you ready for that? Kindergartners have a lot of energy."

"Especially this time of year," he agreed. "Yeah. I can handle it."

"Good. I'm sure your dad is tickled pink you made the offer."

"We could hang out. After the rehearsal."

McKenzie read the hopeful look on his face. Was he feeling something, too? An innocent crush? Attraction? She looked away, though, the nagging feeling that it didn't matter rumbling through her. Duran's life was here; he was close to his family, and he liked living in Amesbury. Her life was over a thousand miles away. As interested as she might be in pursuing something with Duran, McKenzie wasn't willing to give up her life at home or her career—the one she had finally started.

"I'd like that," she answered sincerely. Because even if there was no chance she and Duran would date, no chance they would ever be an item, they could be friends. McKenzie cherished all her friendships; making friends in her adult life was a blessing.

Over dinner, they talked about the kindergartners Duran would be corralling all weekend. While he seemed very aware that he had his work cut out for him, it was obvious that he was actually looking forward to it. Just more of the Christmas lover in him, or did he like kids? Did he want to have his own children someday?

The Christmas music played on as they finished eating and McKenzie helped him clear the dishes and clean the kitchen. Still talking and laughing together, she felt at home with him, in his house, and she found herself hoping they would maintain a friendship when she left on Sunday.

Finally, when the clock struck ten, and they had played several hands of rummy, all the while singing along to the familiar songs of the season, McKenzie announced that she should get going. True to his word, Duran insisted he would take her back to the lodge. He offered to drive, but McKenzie preferred the walk.

"I want to soak up as much atmosphere here as I can," she told him as they bundled up in their coats.

Though the temperature had hovered in the mid-twenties all evening, the absence of wind made the walk pleasant. Duran quizzed her about her family, asking about her brother, if she was close to him, if he lived at home, what sorts of trouble the two of them had gotten into when they were kids. McKenzie accused him of pushing the naughty list at her again, but she did admit that she and her brother had never been angels.

"We didn't make it to see the reindeer farm," she said quietly as they passed the reindeer pen on Main Street on their way to the lodge.

"What if we went Saturday night? After the program?" he suggested. "It'll be all lit up. Trust me, you'll love it."

"I'd like that." She glanced up at him.

"It's a date," he said with a nod.

The trouble with that? She wished it was.

CHAPTER SIXTEEN

DURAN

The rehearsal was so bad, Duran was relatively sure the program itself couldn't go any worse. One kid got sick at Duran's feet. While he made the phone calls to have a parent come and get the boy, two others wandered away from the group in the church yard. He caught the boy and girl trying to climb a tree. The little kid he had seen in the gym the day he'd come to talk to his mom started a snowball fight. And the class sounded warbly and sick when they sang their Christmas songs after acting out the nativity scene.

He fibbed to his mom via text later that evening. Told her everything was fine.

"Mrs. Vahle will see the program," she reminded him when he answered her call. "If it tanks, I'll know."

"It's not gonna tank," he told her. "For one thing, they're little kids. Little kids are cute."

"Speaking of cute," she said in a singsong voice.

"No."

"Are you still seeing her?"

"Hanging out, Mom," he corrected her. "We're not together."

"Why not?"

"Because she lives over a thousand miles away."

"And?"

"That's a bit much for a long-distance relationship," he answered. "I don't think either of us has the cash to throw away for weekly plane tickets."

"Amesbury's not the only place to live, Duran."

Before he could make sense of her comment, she continued.

"Send me some pictures of the kids."

"Will do."

"Love you."

"Love you and Dad, too. Have fun."

Maybe her reminder that Mrs. Vahle would see the program since she was currently in rehab at Sedgwick was supposed to make him nervous. If anything, it made him feel better. For one thing, the kids might be better behaved knowing their teacher was in the audience.

For the Friday evening performance for parents and families, Duran enlisted a couple of moms to help him. Although, the kids were much more cooperative for the real thing. Dressed in black pants and white sweatshirts with Rudolph on the front, Duran could almost feel the buzz of their excitement in the air. Unfortunately, their sweatshirts were covered for the entire program outside. First, they were dressed as shepherds, wise men, sheep, an angel, a star, and of course, Mary, Jesus, and Joseph, and once they sang "Silent Night" around the manger the school custodian had made and erected for them, they had to bundle up in coats to finish singing.

Duran's favorite part of the evening wasn't the actual nativity scene, although he did feel ridiculously proud of the boys and girls. The best part of the whole night was looking around the families crowded into the church yard as the kids sang and seeing McKenzie off to the side of the crowd with a smile brighter than any Christmas lights.

He was in trouble. He knew it, but he was helpless to save himself. Other than his relationship with Kaeli in high school, he had never been in love. But something about McKenzie made him wonder. He definitely liked her. He loved her smile, her bright eyes, and her laugh. But he loved talking to her; it felt like he'd known her forever. Duran thought he could sit and talk to her forever and never run out of things to say.

And she was leaving the day after tomorrow.

MRS. VAHLE GAVE HIM A THUMBS UP AFTER THE SATURDAY afternoon program. The kids had acted out the nativity scene perfectly for the residents at the nursing home. Duran was thrilled at how each of the kids enunciated his or her lines so clearly. The shepherds and wise men, even the sheep, cattle, and donkeys had been reverent as the group sang "Away in a Manger." And when the costumes came off, and the kids stood in a group before the residents, they dazzled them with lively renditions of "Rudolph the Red Nosed Reindeer" and "Frosty the Snowman."

Pictures sent to his mom, Duran spent time talking to the kids when the program was finished. Excited for Christmas, for Santa, they yakked his ears off, sharing stories about their houses and trees. Duran listened patiently to all of them and took time to talk to the parents and residents, too.

"Young man," Mrs. Vahle said to him with a big smile. "You saved Christmas."

Duran laughed, a little embarrassed by the praise. "I didn't do anything, Mrs. Vahle."

"Of course you did," she corrected him. "I teach those boys and girls every day. I know how wild they can be."

"It was fun," he told her. "And I know my parents are enjoying themselves. So, it all worked out."

"I appreciate it, Duran," the older woman told him. "What a selfless young man you are to have taken this on."

"Actually, it was my friend's idea," he admitted. He glanced over his shoulder to see McKenzie talking to a few of the kindergarten moms. She nodded when he caught her eye and excused herself to make her way over to stand by him. "Mrs. Vahle, this is my friend McKenzie Noble."

"Thank you, McKenzie." The woman smiled. "You and Duran saved Christmas for a lot of people."

"It's nice to meet you, Mrs. Vahle." McKenzie smiled and touched her arm. "I didn't do anything. Duran did the work."

"You're the pretty little blonde everyone's talking about."

Duran coughed as heat rushed his face.

"I'm here on business." To Duran's relief, McKenzie only smiled at the comment. "Amesbury is a beautiful town."

"Isn't it, though?" Mrs. Vahle quirked an eyebrow at her and then turned that look on Duran.

Time to get away from her, he decided.

"Well, Mrs. Vahle, I'm going to take McKenzie out to the reindeer farm."

"Oh." The woman's smile lit up her face. "Say hello to Casey Kasem for me."

CHAPTER SEVENTEEN

With the blanket of snow on the ground as far as her eyes could see, it looked to McKenzie as if the reindeer farm went on and on until the end of the world. White lights hung in the row of evergreens that lined the front of the property. The house and each of the five barns and outbuildings were also lined with white lights. The glow of the lights on the snow was magical.

As was the case on Main Street, Christmas music played from hidden speakers. Near a smaller outbuilding that Duran explained was used as an equipment shed and not a barn for animals, stood a small white tent. Also lit up, a small evergreen decorated just beside it.

Duran led her there first, explaining she could get eggnog or hot cocoa, as well as candied almonds or homemade sugar cookies. Breathless with wonder for the whole scene, McKenzie didn't even utter a protest about the calories as she chose eggnog and a sugar cookie. When would she ever see something so beautiful, so magical again?

At the back of the equipment shed, people gathered around a fire pit, flames blazing and wood popping invitingly. She and Duran approached and hovered close for a bit. Her front was warm in seconds, but winter pressed in behind her ready to claim her again.

A golden retriever lay stretched out in front of an Adirondack chair, the same kind the lodge patio had featured.

"Is that Casey Kasem?" McKenzie leaned into Duran and whispered.

"It is." He nodded.

"Beautiful dog."

"He is," he agreed. "Wanna walk? Find the reindeer?"

"Yes."

The cold crept in on her the second they moseyed away from the fire, but she didn't care. Her cookie gone, Duran reached for her hand and linked their gloved fingers as he led her toward the barn on the eastern end of the property.

"What do you think?"

"I love it," she answered simply.

"People come here, but you can also go to the tree farm down the road. Same set up. But their dog's name is Hank."

"Nice." She smiled. "This is seriously right out of a movie setting, Duran."

He squeezed her fingers as they neared the entrance to the barn. She smelled the hay, the tang of manure mixed with leather as they entered. There were ten stalls, but only four were currently occupied. She laughed as she and Duran wandered down the center aisle of the barn and she read the crazy reindeer names.

Tom Petty.

Tina Turner.

Kenny Rogers.

Alvin.

"Alvin?" She looked at Duran in askance.

"The Chipmunk."

"Ohmygosh." She laughed and shook her head. "Love it. I love it here."

At the end of the aisle, Duran turned her to face him.

"I wish you could stay."

Eyes locked with his, her heart fell. She wanted to stay here, but she couldn't. Wasn't that part of being an adult? Sure, she loved Amesbury. And she liked Duran. A lot. But she had responsibilities at home. She had family. A job that she loved and wanted very much to succeed at.

"Me, too." She nodded.

"You could come back to visit," he suggested. To take the sting out of the moment, he wiggled his eyebrows and made her laugh. "I mean, sure, for the conference. But you could come and visit me."

"Maybe."

She wanted to promise that she would, but McKenzie didn't make promises she wasn't sure she could keep.

"This wasn't supposed to happen," he said quietly.

"I know. I told myself the same thing."

"I like you," he told her, his low voice thick with emotion.

"Duran," she whispered. "Me, too. But I have to go home."

"I know." He stepped back. McKenzie missed his warmth immediately, though she could breathe easier.

She cleared her throat.

"Can we pet them?"

"Of course."

He followed her as she made her way down the line on one side and then back up the other, talking to each of the reindeer as she stroked their noses. When they left the barn, McKenzie hunched her shoulders and huddled deeper into her coat. It felt much colder outside, but she knew it was simply that she and Duran had acknowledged what might be growing between them.

Acknowledged it and walked away from it.

Reminding herself they had the rest of the night together, she put a smile on her face when they ended up back at the fire pit. A group of little kids started singing "Santa Claus is Coming to Town," and eventually, everyone around the fire joined in.

She was exhausted by the time she and Duran made their way back to his SUV. Warm and cozy inside on the drive back into Amesbury, McKenzie rested her head on the seat and studied Duran's face as he drove.

"How long will your parents be gone?"

"Two weeks."

"They'll be gone over Christmas?"

"Mm-hmm." He nodded. "We'll celebrate in January when they're back home."

She mulled over that information as he turned into the parking lot at the lodge. Drowsy, warm, and comfortable with him, McKenzie hated getting out into the cold again. Duran helped her out of her seat, closed her door, and walked her inside.

"So." She cleared her throat. "What're you doing for Christmas?"

He sighed and shrugged. "Just hanging out at my place. Might see friends if they happen to come home for the holidays."

She nodded and wondered if she was crazy for what she was thinking.

"What if..." She arched her eyebrows hopefully. "You came home with me? For the holidays?"

Duran stared at her silently for a moment.

"What about the store?"

"We're a few days out from Christmas," she said quietly. "Just think about it."

She lowered her eyes over his face and let her gaze linger on his chest.

"It's not as picturesque as Amesbury," she admitted. "But I would love to show you my hometown and share my Christmas with you."

Duran shifted on his feet and drew his forehead into a deep frown.

"Yeah." He nodded. "I will. I'll think about it."

Not convinced, she took a deep breath and nodded.

"Yeah. Okay." She smiled. "I'll...send you my address."

"Okay."

"Just in case."

"Yeah. Great. Good idea."

She hated to walk away, but prolonging this goodbye wasn't going to make anything easier. McKenzie had enjoyed her time in Amesbury, and it was possible she would be back. But she and Duran would never be more than friends.

And rather than be angry or disappointed, she wanted to accept that. She wanted him in her life.

"Goodnight, Duran."

"Goodnight." He leaned toward her and brushed his lips over her forehead.

"Thanks for making this such a special trip."

He took a step away from her and looked at her with a smile.

"Thanks for saving Christmas."

McKenzie laughed and waved as he headed back outside. He wasn't going to think about spending the holiday with her. This was goodbye. They might text. Maybe talk on the phone now and then. And she would look him up if she was back in Amesbury.

But his thank you for saving Christmas was loaded with his goodbye.

Unfortunately, saving Christmas for him, for his parents, for the Amesbury community, had only stolen a little light from her own.

CHAPTER EIGHTEEN

DURAN

The store was closed on Sundays, always had been. And while they were open until three in the afternoon on Christmas Eve, they weren't usually busy. They had an occasional local rush in to grab something small, a stocking stuffer maybe. But he and his dad had joked about spending more money to turn the lights on for Christmas Eve than they earned in that short amount of time.

He had stayed up late the night before. Wasn't tired. Knew he wouldn't sleep. After he had left McKenzie at the lodge, he had driven straight home. Changed from his warm boots and sweater into flannel pajama pants and crashed in his recliner to watch movies.

Rather than watch the regulars he and his parents watched year after year, he watched *Die Hard*. Channel-surfed for a bit before settling on an old black and white cowboy movie. And finally hit the streaming services for something to keep his mind off McKenzie.

When he did finally go to bed, he tossed and turned. The last time he looked at the clock, it was nearly three. Duran wasn't the type of guy to worry, to second guess himself. But as he tossed and turned, he second and third and fourth guessed his plans to stay in Amesbury. To work with his dad. To take over the store. His dad had never said he expected that of him, but Duran had worked with him at the store since he was thirteen. They worked well together.

But his dad, his parents weren't his future. Sure, he wanted years and years of the future *with* them. But one day, they would be gone. And Duran would be alone.

Like he was now.

Maybe he wouldn't have given it a thought, if he hadn't met McKenzie.

He hadn't set an alarm, so he woke to the sound of his phone vibrating on the nightstand. With an irrational hope that it was McKenzie telling him she changed her mind and wanted to stay, he lunged for it and snatched it up.

The number on the screen was his mom's.

"Hi."

"Hey. I spoke with Mrs. Vahle last night," she announced. "She said you did a fantastic job."

"Yeah." He sighed and stacked his free hand under his head. Studied the ceiling above his bed. "The kids did a good job."

"And you're not taking credit?" his mom teased.

"I think it would be like a substitute taking credit for a class doing well on final exams," he said simply.

"Well, you sound grumpy."

"Just tired."

"Didn't you sleep?"

"Actually, no. Not well."

He pulled that same hand from under his head now and rubbed at his eyes.

"What's wrong?"

Duran sighed. No use in telling her now. His parents were on vacation. They didn't need to worry about him. His dad might never forgive him if he gave his mom something else to stew over while they were gone.

"Nothing."

"Duran Carey. What is going on?"

He groaned as he sat up. A glance at his alarm clock told him it was after nine.

"McKenzie goes home today."

"Oh."

"Yeah. So...I don't know. It was fun."

"Will you keep in touch?"

"Maybe. I dunno." He climbed out of bed and padded bare-foot to the kitchen. "She asked me to come home with her for Christmas."

He pulled the refrigerator door open and selected the orange juice. Banged that door closed and took a glass from the cabinet by the sink.

"Well, that's great! When do you leave?"

"I'm not going, Mom."

"Why wouldn't you go?"

"What about the store?"

"You can close Christmas Eve, Duran. You can close for a few days. It's a family run business."

Ignoring the juice and the glass, he leaned his back on the counter and scrubbed his fingers through his hair.

"You're acting like your mother," his dad announced. Duran cringed realizing his mom must have put him on speaker phone. "Of course you can take some time off and enjoy yourself."

"But what's the point?" he asked, sounding every bit the sullen, grumpy kid he felt like right now. "We live way too far apart to think we could make it work. And she loves her job. I can't ask her to give that up."

"What if you followed her?" his mom suggested.

"What?"

"You have a business degree, Duran. You're helping me run a store. You have potential you haven't even tapped yet. What if she's the one?"

"Dad—"

"Now, I'm not saying propose on Christmas Eve." His dad continued. "But what if she's the one? And you miss out on this opportunity? She wants you to spend Christmas with her. That's quite a gift, son."

Duran swallowed hard.

"And if she's not the one?"

"So, you spend Christmas with a friend. You haven't taken time off from the store since you came back from college. I think Amesbury can do without Slopes for a week."

⁂

MCKENZIE HAD TOLD HIM HER FLIGHT WAS AT FIVE. HE HAD QUITE a drive to the airport, so once he got off the phone with his parents, he hurried through a shower and packed his bag. Duran didn't cross his fingers, but he sure hoped as he left Amesbury that he would catch her at the airport.

That her offer to come home with her for Christmas was still good.

On the drive, he thought about calling her. But he was nervous, a bit afraid that she would revoke the offer. Uninvite him. Not that he wanted her to hold the offer open out of guilt when he showed up at the airport.

He would know. If she was sincere, if she wanted him to go with her, he would know. Which made him wonder if his dad knew something he didn't. What if she *was* the one? It had happened fast, but then, didn't every couple have *that moment*? The spark that drew them together? He didn't have to rush into anything, but it couldn't hurt to spend more time with her.

Christmas music kept him company until he was fifteen minutes from the airport. Then he was nervous again, and he had to turn the radio off so he could think. Worry.

The airport, thankfully, was small. Crowded, but if McKenzie was here, he would find her. It wasn't quite three thirty, so he assumed she would be here, checked in for her flight. But he had to purchase a ticket to get through security. Gambling had never been his sport, but Duran swiped his credit card with a flourish, thanked the woman at the ticket counter, and went in search of Gate Seven.

Every seat at the gate was taken. Duran scanned the faces, the heads lowered over open books or laptops. The building was warm, so most people had taken their coats off. But Duran looked for her pretty blond hair rather than the bright red coat. He found her sitting by the window, eyes on a book.

Not the Ford Bishop book, from what he could tell. He approached her slowly. The paperback had black on the cover, which made him assume it was a thriller.

"Excuse me, miss, is that a Zeke Kannard book you're reading?" He stood before her, praying his knees didn't give out as he waited for her to look up at him.

"Duran?" she whispered as she closed the book. Did the fact that it was a Zeke Kannard book mean anything? Zeke Kannard was definitely in his top three favorite writers. Hers too?

"Hey."

She stood slowly and put the book on her seat. "What're you doing here?" She shook her head and took in the suitcase at his side. "How'd you get through security?"

"Bought a plane ticket," he answered simply.

"Where—? But where're you—what about the store?"

"Slopes will be closed for the holidays. All week." He swallowed hard as their eyes met. "Because a pretty little blond invited me to come home with her for Christmas."

Her lips formed a perfect O of surprise.

"You're coming with me?"

"Am I still invited?"

Duran squeezed his eyes closed as she threw herself at him. With her arms around the back of his neck, Duran wrapped his around her waist.

"I take it that's a yes?"

"You just saved my Christmas," she whispered.

He drew back just enough to look her in the eyes again. "Where's the mistletoe when you need it?"

"I don't need it." She shook her head. "But I do want you to kiss me."

Her smile lit him up inside. Everyone around them faded away, the buzz of conversation and the airline announcements sounded a million miles away. Duran cupped her chin in his hand and brushed his lips over hers.

"Merry Christmas, McKenzie."

She nodded, arms still wrapped around his neck. "Merry Christmas, Duran."

EPILOGUE

Four Years Later

"Who needs snow?"

Eyes closed under the straw hat tipped over her face, McKenzie smiled at her brother's question.

"Snowman."

"Sure, but look."

McKenzie lifted her head from the beach chair, tipped the hat up, and peeked at her brother and her daughter. Lily would be three in December. Christian was determined to make her like sand and surf better than snow and Christmas. He had his work cut out for him, considering she and Duran visited Amesbury as often as they could. Duran might live in Illinois now, but the man still loved Christmas.

114

Christian was building a sandman. Lily watched with a frown on her face.

"Santa." She shook her head.

"Santa would find you here," Christian told her.

Lily, blond hair in tiny pigtails, flicked her gaze to McKenzie.

"Santa knows I's at the beach, Mommy?"

"He does," McKenzie promised her. "Help Uncle Christian with the sandman."

"Here you go, babe."

McKenzie looked up as her husband appeared at her side, a cold bottle of water in hand.

"Thank you." She took the bottle, twisted the cap off, and took a long drink.

"Daddy!" Spotting Duran, Lily ran on her chubby legs to him. He leaned over to scoop her up. "Santa's coming."

"Well, yeah," Duran agreed, "but not until Christmas, sweetie. We have a few months to wait. Santa comes after your birthday."

"I want Grampa." Lily wiggled until Duran put her down. McKenzie watched her trudge through the sand to the umbrella where her parents were relaxing. She climbed up on McKenzie's dad's lap and leaned back on his chest. "Unca Chrisshan is naughty."

"Hey!" Christian yelped. He shot a look at McKenzie. "What kind of stories are you feeding her?"

"Truth hurts, bro." McKenzie shrugged.

"Let's walk," Duran suggested and held out his hand. McKenzie took it and let him pull her to her feet.

"Going for a walk," she told her parents so they would know to keep an eye on Lily.

"Dad texted me while I was at the concessions," Duran announced.

"What's up?"

"He found a buyer. For the store."

"Oh." McKenzie looked up, worried that he might be upset. "How do you feel about that?"

Duran squeezed her fingers. "Well, since I love working at Renfield Manufacturing, and since we're not planning to move back to Amesbury any time soon, I think it's great."

"Yeah?"

"Yeah." He stopped walking and turned to her. "Now my parents can travel more. Spend more time together."

"Good." McKenzie nodded. "Works out for everybody."

Duran rubbed the back of his knuckles over her belly, covered by her one-piece swimsuit. "Everybody."

"When should we tell them?" she asked with a grin.

***

Thank you for reading Eggnog in Amesbury! If you enjoyed McKenzie and Duran's story, please consider leaving a review on your favorite bookish site!

TURN THE PAGE TO READ THE FIRST CHAPTER OF FEELS ON WHEELS

CHRISTMAS IN AMESBURY

Introducing Christmas in Amesbury!

If you like romantic comedies that hug you like a warm, fuzzy robe—this is the series to binge. Amesbury, Montana, is the ideal holiday destination—visitors and home towners embrace all the drama, meet cutes, and romance shenanigans.

Series link: https://shorturl.at/ovOX9

HEA guaranteed!

Swoon over the sweet romance.

NINE sweet romance novels with all the tropes you love!

It's every Christmas lover's dream!

SNEAK PEEK AT FEELS ON WHEELS

Chapter 1

Jaws lopes out from the bend of woods on the back edge of the property with a bird flopping in his mouth again. Darn dog. I'd like to think he didn't grab that sucker alive, but I've seen him do it a time or two.

"Jaws." I stick my fingers in my mouth and whistle.

The German Shepherd mix trots a few steps and then puts it in high gear when he sees me.

"Whaddaya doin', bud?" I scratch his ears as he drops the dead bird at my feet. Jaws leans into my hand as I study the bird. Thankfully, this one looks like it's been dead awhile, so I can't blame my dog.

He decides he's had enough love and bounds back toward the woods, stopping on a dime when I whistle at him again.

"Home."

When I yell the word, Jaws drops his head like a little kid, pouting when his mom sends him home. I would know. I played my mom every chance I got when I was a kid. Still do, sometimes. Not my fault she hasn't caught on yet. Either that or she's got a soft spot for me.

I make sure my dog trots to the gravel drive at the side of the woods before starting the weed whacker again. Eyes on the ground, I trim the weeds around the rink's parking area, careful to keep the toes of my work boots out of range.

A car pulls into the lot behind me, and I hear four doors shutting and the excited chatter of little kids mixed with laughter from grown women. Pretty normal on this side of the property. Wolverine Park covers a hundred acres— some of them family friendly and some not. The skating rink, obviously, is for the kids. Plenty of adults go in; plenty of them end up sprawled on their butts with broken bones, too.

I lift my arm to rub the sweat off my face. I forgot I was still wearing the light flannel shirt I put on over my park t-shirt earlier. It was cooler at six in the morning. The late afternoon sun and the work on the grounds is making me warm. Ready to peel the shirt off, I prop the weed whacker on my leg and shrug it off my shoulders.

The noisy kids are racing each other across the gravel lot. I have a few nieces and nephews, and every one of them has crashed and burned there.

"Bryson!" One of the women calls. Both boys stop and turn to look, sliding a few inches on the gravel. Neither wipes out, but the woman tells them not to run. When the boys take off again, first at a fast walk and then, of course, at a run again, the other woman nudges the first with her elbow.

"Seriously? You think they're gonna listen?"

They're dressed in skinny jeans and those slip-on loafer sneakers that are all the rage right now. My sister has four pairs. Hair pulled up in nearly matching ponytails, the women look enough like twins that they have to be sisters.

Interesting. Maybe I should tell my brother we should dress alike. Truman would love that. The snort I make at the thought draws their attention to me.

"Hi." I nod and watch them walk by with their pale pink lips tipped up in smiles. If either of them wears makeup, it's light and natural. They say hi and keep going, one of them bumping into the mirror on the side of a car parked by the door—hard enough that she bounced off.

Ouch. Bet that hurt. I flinch and look away as I hear an ouch and a groan.

I see a lot of people around the family fun park. Most are friendly and talkative. We get a lot of locals, as the place has been here for over twelve years. It's changed a lot, hopefully for the better. Since I took the helm, we've grown the place into a major tourist attraction. Took some work. The zoning was right, but some locals fought us on the expansion and the update to the current attractions. Mostly, they're over that now. Parts of Wolverine Park are open year-round, so those tourist dollars are pretty steady all year long.

We keep it looking nice, too. I'm meticulous about the grounds and the buildings. The landscaping is always well-kept, paint's always fresh, and the interiors of the buildings are neat and inviting. It's not even so much that I want to keep the city officials from breathing down my neck. It's just who I am. My daddy taught me pride of ownership.

Granted, I got started on Daddy's dime, but I went to school, and I worked my butt off on several jobs during those years and after. I worked for Daddy, too, and I socked all that money away. I don't need much. I've got an old farmhouse at the back edge of the property where I live with Jaws—didn't pay for him. He's a stray that wandered down my drive a couple of years ago. I fed him and bathed him when he stuck around for a few days. No collar. No tags. No chip. He must have decided he liked me alright, because he stuck around.

Jaws and I drive an old Chevy pickup that's got some miles on it. Still runs. Perfect for me. My siblings are both high maintenance people; they take after our father. Apparently, the middle child—me—got my maternal grandfather's personality. My simple life leaves Truman and Harper baffled.

I put the weed whacker back on the trailer and eye the land around the rink. Looks good. Most people are surprised I don't hire this stuff out. The groundskeeping alone here is a full-time job. But it's what I do. It's what I *want* to do. I check to make sure the tractor is secure on the trailer and then climb into the truck. I need to get this equipment put away and check one of the faucets in the girls' bathroom at the rink.

Mila Fuentes, my second-in-command, lifts her chin in my direction when I park the truck in front of the garage—also always well-kept and neat. I jump out of the truck and head back to the hitch.

"Pax is working on the a/c unit in number one." She bends back over the chassis of another trailer. Like me, Mila is a jack-of-all-trades. She peeks at me now, and I notice a steak of oil and dirt on her face. The difference being she cleans up and looks good in a dress. Then again, I've never tried one, so who knows what I'd look like in one.

"Good." I release the lock mechanisms and the safety pins and then go back to the cab of the truck to jockey it around enough to loosen the hitch. "I'm gonna go take care of that faucet Nadine called about earlier."

"What's for dinner?" Mila asks me.

"Mom's pot roast," I tell her, savoring both the thought of the dinner plate Mom left and Mila's jealous eye roll. "C'mon over. There's plenty." She knows this. Mom babies me way more than she babies Truman. Must be the middle child thing. Or maybe she just likes me better—that's what I tell Truman, anyway.

"Got a date," Mila answers.

"Oh yeah? That's cool." I jump back down from the truck and check the hitch again.

"Going to Charter's."

"Why would you go there when you know food and service is better right here at the Cabin?"

"You don't bring your dates around here."

With the hitch released, I go back to the cab of the truck, but I lean around my open door to look at Mila.

"I don't date."

***

If you would like to read more of Twain and Mabry's story, click here:

Feels on Wheels

ALSO BY TRACY BROEMMER

Women's Fiction Novels:

Luther's Cross (10th Anniversary Edition)

Fairytale (Writing as Therese Kinkaide)

Just Like Them

Small Hours

Picket Fences

Two Story Home

Green-Eyed Girl

Say Everything

Come Home for Christmas

Sketching Litchfield Lake

Ever, Again

Safe as Houses

Damsel

The Valentine Suite

Women's Fiction Series in Order

Lorelei Bluffs

Every Little Thing

Two A.M.

Blind

Leaving July

Hesitation Marks

Four Letter Words

See Kate

Loved You More

A Lorelei Ending

I Do

The Williams Legacy

Truth Is

Other People's Ugly

Omissions

Women's Fiction Short Stories

India Falls

Luther's Cross: 87,600

The Candy Cane Tree of Willow Lane

Delays

Same Time Next Year

Contemporary Romance Novels

Destiny's Calling: Your Future is Waiting

Wedding Day Shenanigans

Holiday Fling

The Kiss Off

Something Like Love

Plus One

End in Flames

Contemporary Romance Series In Order

The Mississippi Queen Trilogy

Love, Nashville

Forever, Duncan

Always, Jess

Truly, Dante (A Short Story)

The H Books

Gettin' Hitched

Hookin' Up'

Holdin' On (A Novella)

Timberton Hounds (Novellas)

Priceless Memory (A Short Story)

Endless Summer

Homeless Holiday

Restless Hearts (Currently included in Fall Into Love, an anthology by Fluffy Fox Publishing)

515 Whiskey

Intoxicate Me (A Novella)

Taste Me

Kissing Springs Trio

Shameless Santa

Sunshine & Soulmates

Bourbon & Bedposts

Lockland Distilling: Keys to Love Trilogy & Kissing Springs World

Leaving You (A Short Story)

Seducing You (A Novella)

Kissing You (A Novella—currently included in the Let's Get Naughty, Volume 2)

Shared World Novels

Hold Onto the Stars (Blue Collar Romance Series, Book #5)

The Jane Thing (Meet Cute Book Club Series, Book #2)

Shameless Santa (Welcome to Kissing Springs, Book #7)

Doctor Divine (Doctors of Eastport, Season 2)

Sunshine & Soulmates (Welcome to Kissing Springs, Book #

Bourbon & Bedposts (Welcome to Kissing Springs, Book #

Moonlight in Montreal (The Vagabond Series)

Beach Daze (Flamingo Island)

Christmas & Other Inconveniences (Betting on Christmas Collection)

Love in Motion Duet (Novellas)

Feels on Wheels

Rings on Wings

The Wine Tasting Series (Short Romantic Stories)

Perfect Pictures (Traminette)

Coming Home (Edelweiss)

Save Me Every Dance (Rosé)

Marry Me (Shiraz)

Birthday Wishes (Muscat)

Dad Jeans (Vignoles)

Contemporary Romance Novellas

Boone's Girl

Today, Again

Indian Summer

Dear Jaclyn Perris

Mistletoe Mishaps

Deadman's Hollow

French Stuff

Holdin' On

Toasted

End in Flames

Endless Summer

Homeless Holiday

Feels on Wheels

Rings on Wings

Intoxicate Me

Contemporary Romance Short Stories

Truest Love (Currently included in Show of Dreams anthology)

Swipe for Fangs (Currently included in the anthology Welcome to Whynot)

Mrs. Bennett

Peppermint Lane

The Principles of Accounting

Strawberry Wine

Love Letter

Sambuca Santa

Truly Dante

Leaving You

Priceless Memory

Perfect Pictures (Traminette)

Coming Home (Edelweiss)

Save Me Every Dance (Rosé)

Marry Me (Shiraz)

Birthday Wishes (Muscat)

Dad Jeans (Vignoles)

Other Novellas

The Devy Man, A Horror Novella

The Keeper's Heart, A Horror Novella

Anthologies

Just Coffee — French Stuff (2020)

Snowed Inn, Vol. 1 — Holdin' On (2020)

Aced, Back to School — Boone's Girl (2021)

Snowed Inn, Vol. 2 — Delays (2021)

Sweet Treats — Peppermint Lane (2021)

Sweet Sprinkles — Same Time Next Year (2022)

Rescue Me — End in Flames (2022)

Fall Into Love — Feels on Wheels (2022)

Cool Off — Endless Summer (2022)

Fall Back Into Love — Rings on Wings (2022)

Backing the Bluegrass — Leaving You (2022)

Kissing Santa Claus — Sambuca Santa (2022)

Let's Get Naughty — Homeless Holiday (2022)

XOXO — Trusting Cupid (2023)

Mrs. Right — Mrs. Bennett (2023)

Tease Me — Taste Me (2023)

Falling for the Boss — The Principles of Accounting (2023)

Ride a Cowboy — Seducing You (2023)

Love and Coffee — Makin' Whoopsie! (2023)

Fall Into Love — Restless Hearts (2023)

Welcome to Whynot — Swipe for Fangs (2023)

Let's Get Naughty, Volume 2 — Kissing You (2023)

Show of Dreams — Truest Love

ABOUT THE AUTHOR

Tracy Broemmer is the author of several contemporary romance novels including Destiny's Calling, Plus One, and the Love in Motion Duet. Tracy also writes women's fiction and is the author of the Williams Legacy series as well as several stand-alone titles.

Tracy's books have been called gripping, emotional, and timely, and readers describe her characters as real and relatable.

Tracy lives in Midwestern Illinois with her husband of 30 years. Visit her on the web and sign up for her newsletter at www.broemmerbooks.com